MOON GRIEVED

Mirror Lake Wolves - Book Five

JENNIFER SNYDER

MOON GRIEVED
MIRROR LAKE WOLVES – BOOK FIVE

© 2018 by Jennifer Snyder
Editing by H. Danielle Crabtree
© 2018 Cover Art by Cora Graphics
© Shutterstock.com

PROLOGUE

Another scream echoed through the building. It was less shrill, less sharp than before. Whoever had screamed was growing weaker by the second.

I blew out my candles without making a wish and raced to the door behind everyone else. My feet faltered when I saw who had screamed. A girl. Dressed in a white nightgown. She stumbled toward us. Her long black hair fell to her waist in a disheveled mess. Mascara was smudged beneath her eyes, and her ashen skin appeared slick with sweat. Her plump lips formed the shape of an O as though she were struggling to scream but unable to make a sound.

My heart hammered hard and fast inside my chest, not because of her presence or the eeriness emanating from her looks, but because of the blood soaking the neckline of her nightgown.

I didn't have to step closer to her to know I'd find two

puncture marks on her throat. I also didn't have to guess any longer if the Midnight Reaper would make his way to Mirror Lake.

Standing there I already knew the answer to both questions, and it was enough to send my mind racing as fast as my heart. The Midnight Reaper was here, and this was one of his victims.

Happy freaking birthday to me.

1

My alarm sounded, startling me awake. I reached out from underneath my blankets to pound the top of it and stop the incessant beeping.

It was early. Too early.

"It can't be morning yet," Eli grumbled from beside me. "What time did you set that thing for?"

"Six." I yawned.

"*Six*? Why are you getting up so damn early?"

I sat up in bed and smoothed my fingers through my tangled hair. "I switched shifts with Pamela. Remember? One of her kids had something at school she needed to be there for this morning." Another yawn pushed its way from me. God, why had I agreed to work her shift at Rosemary's? Getting up this early was torture. How did she do this every day? "I'll be back on the dinner shift after this. It's only one morning. " My last words were said more for my benefit than Eli's. No part of me enjoyed getting up before the sun.

Eli's arm snaked out to wrap around my waist. "You mean we won't be able to cuddle before you go in today?"

"Nope." I attempted to peel out of his grasp, but he'd latched on tight.

I had thirty minutes to get to work; I didn't have the time to cuddle with Eli the way he wanted.

"Aw, man. Do we at least get to eat breakfast together?" Eli asked as he struggled to maintain his grip on me.

"Not this morning." When I pried his final finger off my hip, he reached out for me again. I laughed. Mornings with him would never grow old. "I have to go. Seriously. You're going to make me late. I need to shower, or else I'm never going to wake up."

"Want some company?"

Temptation tingled through me, but I knew the wise answer to his question, even if my body wanted to say another. "Not a good idea," I said as I slipped out of bed.

"Wrong. It's a great idea."

I glanced at him. Opting to humor him a little, I asked, "Why is that?"

"It saves water, which means we're saving the planet one shower together at a time," he said. A sexy smirk twisted across his face.

"Still not a good idea."

"Give me one good reason." His smirk grew.

"Because you have ways of distracting me, ways that make time cease to exist."

"You say that like it's a bad thing." His tone implied he was pleased with himself.

"When I have to get to work, it is. Leon already doesn't care for me. I don't need to give him another reason."

I had no idea why the cook hated me so much, but he'd made it clear I was by no means his favorite person.

"How could anyone not like you?" he asked as his eyes skimmed my barely clothed body. "You're smart, sexy, and sassy."

I rolled my eyes, knowing what he was trying to pull. It wasn't going to work.

"Why don't you ask him?" I crossed to our dresser and gathered my uniform.

Leon was human. I could sense it. I could also sense he knew nothing of the supernatural world. He was a grouchy hick. One who seemed to loathe any generation younger than his.

I didn't let it bother me much because I needed this job.

Hell, I wanted this job. I'd never been allowed to work a real job before. It was only because I'd imprinted with Eli that I was allowed to. Gran wouldn't have approved of me working a part-time job while attending college.

Now that Eli and I were imprinted and living together, Gran didn't have a say. Thank goodness.

"He'll come around," Eli said as he propped himself up on his elbows in bed. "You're likable...when you smile." He winked.

"What? I smile all the time."

"Uh, huh. Like you are right now?"

"Whatever." I chuckled as I headed toward the hall.

"I smile all the time at work. It's how I make such good tips."

"No," Eli shouted after me. "You're hot. That's how you make such good tips."

I closed the bathroom door and peeled off my tank top and panties. Rosemary's Diner wasn't a place I'd ever thought I would work. It was too bright and busy. People weren't my thing—nature and quiet places were—but out of the five places I'd applied they'd been the only one to call back.

It was a job—even if the cook hated me.

I ran through everything I knew about Leon as I stood beneath the hot water. He was older, probably close to the same age as Gran. His wife's name had been Florence. She'd passed away a few years ago. I didn't know him well enough to know if he'd always been a grump, or if her death had pushed him over the edge.

When I climbed out of the shower, I toweled off and dressed quickly. I swiped on some mascara and ran my fingers through my hair. My time was limited, so it would have to air dry. I left my dirty clothes on the floor, making a mental note to pick them up later, and I headed to the kitchen for something to eat.

Eli was on the couch, a bowl of cereal in his hand and Moonshine tucked into his side, when I stepped into the living room. The TV was on and the voice of a news anchor blasted through the trailer. If I hadn't been awake after my shower, the sound of the reporter's shrill voice would've done the job. She had one of those nails-on-a-chalkboard type of voices that had me gritting my teeth.

"Since when do you watch the news?" I asked Eli as I poured myself a bowl of cereal.

"Since my dad started hounding me about not paying enough attention to things happening."

"Oh." That made sense.

Sometimes, I forgot Eli was the son of our alpha. Moments like this, when he mentioned his dad asking him to do something that correlated with becoming alpha, made me remember.

"So, anything happening?" I asked as I poured milk in my bowl.

"Always." I understood the bitter tone to his words. I'd never enjoyed watching the news. They never reported the good things that happened, only the bad. It was too much negativity for me to handle, especially first thing in the morning.

Against my better judgment, I tuned into what the reporter was saying. Her words shook as though she was upset when she spoke.

"Police were called at around 3 a.m. to Rightmore Street, just south of West Meadow, where another incident was reported two nights ago," she said. "The bodies of Estelle Bright and Claire Holbrooks were discovered there. Investigators believe the two young women are the latest victims of the Midnight Reaper, who has been wreaking havoc across the nation since the beginning of the month."

"Are you kidding me?" I muttered.

"I know. This guy is totally out of hand. He seems to be killing more frequently," Eli said around a mouthful of cereal.

"What happens when he decides to move on from the city? Mirror Lake will probably be the first place he goes, considering its proximity." My gut twisted. The more I thought about it, the more likely it seemed the killer would head here next.

"Even if he did, I doubt he'd be here long. Mirror Lake doesn't have as much potential as the city does for new victims. It would be stupid of him to come here. I mean, he would most likely be caught in a day or two. We're a small community. You can't get away with what he's doing here."

Eli had a point, but my nerves still refused to settle. I had a bad feeling, and Gran always told me to trust my gut.

"Have they released how he's killing his victims?" I asked, unsure if I wanted to know the answer to my question.

"I don't think that's something they release to the public. Knowing wouldn't do any good. It would only cause panic."

Something shifted across Eli's face that made me think he knew more than he was letting on.

"I don't see why that would cause a panic," I said as I stared at him.

I understood he was the alpha's son, but I was his wife, his mate for lack of a better word. He should tell me everything. Including pack-related issues he learned from his father. I hated when he kept me in the dark.

Hadn't I proven over the last few months I was as dedicated to this pack as he was?

Eli's green eyes lifted to meet mine. He'd caught on

that I knew he was keeping something from me in regards to this case. "It's a serial killer, Mina. You don't give away their MO. It's pretty much the only leverage the police have in cases like this." His gaze drifted back to the TV.

My eyes remained on him as I took another bite of my cereal. He was definitely hiding something. I could sense it.

"Just like other victims of the Midnight Reaper, the young women's bodies were found mutilated," the reporter said.

I nearly choked. Mutilated? As in something had attacked them, ripping them to shreds? Something animalistic?

My mind shifted through everything I knew that went bump in the night in the supernatural world, and a shiver slipped down my spine.

"I don't think she meant to say that," Eli insisted, his gaze glued to the TV.

I didn't speak; the reporter's words were on a loop in my mind. She'd used the word *mutilated*. Was that her word to describe what the victims looked like, or was it one she'd heard a police officer use?

The unease in my gut spread. I had a feeling whoever, or whatever, had been tearing up the nation was supernatural. Not only that, but also that he was headed this way.

2

I tried to force what I'd heard about the latest Midnight Reaper killing out of my head, but it was impossible. The word mutilated haunted me throughout the day, bringing up thoughts of the serial killer and what he might actually be.

Was he a vampire? A pissed off rogue werewolf? Something else entirely?

I wasn't the only one thinking of the latest killings; it seemed everyone at Rosemary's Diner had it on their mind as well. The place had been abuzz all morning with the news. People were speculating over their breakfast and morning coffee as to what the Midnight Reaper's motive might be.

Satanic ritual killings were what the majority were saying. That could be because we were in the Bible belt, and anything out of the ordinary was often viewed as satanic here.

I wished that were the case in this situation. A

human performing ritualistic killings would be easier to stop than a crazed supernatural.

My hand shook as I reached for the pot of coffee on the warmer and made my rounds. I'd made it halfway around the diner before I heard something about the killings that caused me to come to a standstill. It came from the town's biggest gossips, who occupied the table near the window, but it didn't mean there wasn't any truth to the woman's words.

"Yes, she said it was Thelma's youngest daughter's best friend. She was in the city and saw the whole thing happen right in front of her. What she was doing in the city alone at that time of night, I have no clue, but she was there. She saw it all," an elderly woman in a blue paisley print dress whispered to the others at the table. "According to Thelma, the poor dear hasn't stepped out of her bedroom since she was brought home. She's scared to death. Said she thought the monster would find her. Thelma said the girl claimed the Midnight Reaper looked into her soul and marked her for death. Claimed he knows her biggest fears now, that he was able to get inside her head."

"Oh, I don't believe that," another of the three women said. She waved the other woman's words away.

"It's true. Jane," the woman in the blue dress said. She placed a wrinkled finger to her lips as though thinking. "Hawker. Jane Hawker. That was her name!"

"Hawker?" the third woman at the table said as I circled around to refill her mug.

I tried to think of anyone with the name Hawker that I knew while at the same time listening to the rest of their conversation. I needed to know more; this girl had supposedly seen who the Midnight Reaper was. She'd referred to him as a monster. Did that mean he was a supernatural as I suspected?

"You know the Hawkers. They live down on Foxfire Lane," the woman in the blue dress said as she ignored me refilling their coffees. "Hatcher and Fiona? The ones with all those kids? I swear, they've got about seven or eight. The younger ones are homeschooled, but what I've heard is once they reach middle school they send them to the public school system. I guess they aren't qualified to teach higher education. Anyway, Jane is one of the middle children. Apparently, she was in the city with some friends when all of this happened. She took a wrong turn down an alley and saw it all. The police found her huddled next to a dumpster. Said she was in shock. Barely even knew her own name."

"Poor thing," one of the older women muttered. "What did she have to say to the police?"

"From what Thelma said, she didn't have much to say at all. Still in shock, I believe. They've tried to call in a specialist to speak with her and see if they could get any information out of her. Apparently, the girl is a little dramatic and has been making up fantastical stories of things she saw that couldn't possibly be true."

I wanted to know these stories. Maybe there was some truth to them, and the old biddies were too closed-minded to notice.

"What were the stories?" one of the women asked. Thankfully.

I placed the coffee pot on an empty table behind

them and swept crumbs from their table into my hand, eager to hear more.

"She said he got in her head. Made her see things," the old woman whispered with dramatic flair before she took a bite her French toast and noticed me hovering. I moved to the table beside them and reached for the coffee pot. Her attention drifted back to her friends. "At least that's what Thelma said."

"Well, there's no doubt she thought it was a monster," another of the three said. "Only a monster could do what was done to those poor young women. It absolutely sickens me."

"Me too. I don't know what's wrong with the world today," another said. "Back when we were young, people didn't mutilate others."

"Oh, I know," the woman in the blue dress chimed in. "We were brought up in a much simpler time. One where no one would even dream of mutilating someone else let alone rampaging across the city while doing so."

"Across the U.S.," another woman corrected her.

"What do you mean?" the woman in the blue dress asked.

"I mean, you should be watching more than the local news. You should be watching the world news. Bob watches it every evening. Normally, I tune it out while I knit, but lately it's been harder with talk of everything that's going on. This killer, this Midnight Reaper, hasn't been only terrorizing the city; he's also done so across the U.S. They've linked cases to him from all over now."

"Why haven't they mentioned any of this on the local news?"

"Because it's not something they want broadcasted yet. There's still investigating to do. At least that's what Bob says. It doesn't make sense to me, though."

"Maybe they are worried about causing hysteria in the public," I suggested without realizing I'd opened my mouth.

The three women looked at me as though I was the rudest person they'd ever encountered.

"It wouldn't cause hysteria," the woman in the blue dress snapped. Clearly, she wasn't a fan of eavesdroppers, even though she most likely was one herself. "Shouldn't you be doing something else besides listening to others' conversations?"

I blinked at her harshness and then walked away, heading toward the kitchen without uttering an apology.

Jane Hawker.

I didn't know her, but it seemed as though I should. Maybe I could persuade Eli into paying her a visit with me. He had to suspect something more sinister at play.

This wasn't a human we were dealing with. It was a supernatural monster, and it seemed as though Jane Hawker knew something about him, something that scared me more than I cared to admit.

He could get inside people's minds.

If that didn't scream supernatural, I don't know what did.

I placed the coffee pot back on its warmer and glanced at Leon. He wasn't looking at me, so I pulled out my cell and browsed the internet looking for mentions of the Midnight Reaper. It didn't take me long to realize the woman in the blue dress had been right. The killings *had* happened across the U.S. I faintly remembered the news anchor this morning mentioning something to that effect as well. Also, if you looked closely at the pattern, it seemed he'd been heading straight for Mirror Lake the entire time.

3

After my shift ended I placed an order for two sandwiches, deciding I'd pay Eli at visit at his work. His shift at the bar had most likely just begun, but I knew Eli was always hungry. He wouldn't turn down food, which meant I'd have time to discuss Jane Hawker and the things I'd overheard with him before the place got too busy.

Eli would want to visit her. He would see things my way and would understand the importance of talking with her. He believed in my gut feelings.

I parked in front of Eddie's bar and cut the engine of my car. The place had just opened, but there were already three vehicles in the parking lot. Regulars. They'd be sitting at one end of the bar with a beer in hand, chatting about old times while smoking a cigarette.

I gathered our sandwiches and drinks before heading toward the entrance of Eddie's. The stale scent of cigarette smoke hung in the air. It grew stronger the closer to the screen door I got. It was a familiar scent, one I'd grown accustomed to long ago. Something I wasn't used to was not coming here daily to pick up my dad after he'd had a few too many.

Since Mom had come home, Dad's drinking had drastically decreased. Actually, he'd gone from getting shitfaced daily to not having a drop in weeks. I didn't know how; alcohol had been the way he dealt with his pain from the accident he was involved in years ago, his version of pain management.

Dad was doing amazing though. Especially considering the medication he was on didn't work as well as it should due to his werewolf healing abilities. They made him metabolize the medication too fast.

The screen door creaked as I pushed it open and slipped inside the dimly lit bar. Cigarette smoke hung suspended in the air like white snakes, and low music played from a speaker in the ceiling.

"Mina Ryan, aren't you ever a sight for sore eyes," Eddie, the owner of the bar, said as the door slammed shut behind me. "Did you bring me lunch?"

"No, sorry, Eddie. I should have. Next time." I smiled as I glanced around the place. "Eli around?" I asked when I didn't see him.

"Sure is," Eddie said. He motioned to the door behind him with his thumb. "He's in the back, washing glasses."

"Care if I take this to him? I know he's supposed to be on the clock, but I promise I won't be in his hair for long."

"It's fine. The boy needs to eat. Besides, it ain't like I

got anything more than pork rinds and peanuts sitting around anyway."

"Thanks." I made my way behind the bar to the back door of the place.

"How's that dad of yours doin'?" Eddie asked when I reached the door.

"Yeah. We haven't seen him 'round here in a while," an older man whose name was Jimbo said. His voice was rough from smoking too many cigarettes in his life.

I glanced at him. He wiped white foam from his upper lip. "He's good," I said, meaning it.

Every time I said the words, pride swelled in me. There weren't many people who could go cold turkey the way he had and not become a complete asshole to everyone close to them.

Dad wasn't perfect, but he was pleasant to be around.

Maybe not every day. Maybe not every second. But he was still in good spirits, and it had everything to do with Mom being back.

He'd been lost without her.

"Still sober?" Eddie asked. A skeptical gleam entered his eyes.

"Still sober," I said.

Eddie broke into a smile. "Damn. I sure am proud of him."

"We all are," I said.

"Never would have thought someone like him would've gone cold turkey," Jimbo said as he puffed on a cigarette. "Shoot, I figured he would've drunk till the day he died."

"Which is what you plan on doin', ain't it?" Eddie asked him with a chuckle.

"Damn straight," Jimbo replied. He flashed a toothless grin and lifted his frothy beer as though he were saluting Eddie's words.

"You weren't the only one who thought he'd drink until the day he died," I admitted. My voice was flat as old emotions flooded me.

"I'm sure his new take on life has everything to do with your mama comin' back to town. I don't know the whole story, but I sure am glad her and the rest of them who seemed to have been gone for so long returned the way they did," Eddie said. More skepticism pooled through his eyes, and I was forced to look away.

Most in town didn't comment on the few more residents living in the trailer park now. Maybe it was because they weren't sure what to say, or maybe it was because they knew there was something more to their return.

Something supernatural.

This wasn't the first time I'd thought Eddie might know what those of us living in the trailer park were. Still, I didn't give him any inkling.

"It does. It has everything to do with my mom's appearance in our lives again," I said as I let myself into the back where Eli was supposed to be washing glasses. I could feel Eddie's gaze on me through the solid door.

I pulled in a deep breath and exhaled as I stepped around boxes, searching for Eli. He was near the far wall, standing at the sink. Oldies music played from a speaker. It wasn't Eli's choice of music, but he still whistled along.

"I didn't know you were an Aretha Franklin kind of

guy," I said as I started toward him. He shifted to face me, a wide grin on his face.

"What are you doing here?" Eli's green eyes lit up at the sight of me.

"Well, hello to you too," I teased.

"Hey." He set the shot glass he'd been washing on the counter and dried his hands on a nearby dishtowel. "Sorry. I'm glad you're here. I'm just surprised is all. And, what's this?" He pointed to the Rosemary's Diner bag in my hand.

"Lunch." I held it out to him. "I got you a turkey club with extra bacon."

"Chips?"

"Of course."

Eli rummaged through the bag until he found his chips. He loved Doritos. "Want to step outside and eat with me? I don't think Eddie will mind."

"He won't," I said as I followed him to the back door of the place. "I talked to him when I came in."

"Awesome, then let's eat."

Eli pushed the back door open and stepped out onto a tiny strip of gravel that butted up against the woods. Warm sunshine beamed down on us as he handed me my sandwich.

"So, what made you think to bring me lunch?" He passed me my chips. "Everything okay?"

It was no surprise he could tell something was bothering me. It was part of our connection, our imprinting. Eli was more in tune with me than I was with myself sometimes.

My mind circled back to what I overheard the older women talking about at the diner.

"Jane Hawker," I said, deciding to get straight to the point. "Do you know her?"

Eli took a bite of his sandwich before answering. "I don't think so. Should I?"

"She's a couple of years younger than me."

"Then, I probably don't know her. Unless she's someone Tate dated."

I shook my head. "No, I don't think he did."

"What about her?"

I tore a piece of bread from my sandwich and placed it in my mouth without meeting his gaze. "I think she knows something about the killings that happened in the city the other night."

"Why do you think that?" His eyes were fixed on me. I knew he was picking apart my words and focusing on my expression.

"I heard a group of older women talking in the diner this morning about her. They said she was a witness. Apparently, she saw everything and is in shock."

"That's awful."

"It is awful. She said she saw a monster. The police questioned her," I said, keeping my eyes glued to Eli, waiting for him to understand where I was going with this. "Supposedly, she locked herself in her bedroom and is refusing to come out. She said the Midnight Reaper is a monster who saw into her soul and claims it will be coming for her next."

Eli stared at me. He understood now. It was clear from the expression twisting his face.

"It's normal for anyone who saw someone murdered to think they saw a monster performing the act."

"What if it was a vampire? Or a rogue werewolf? What if it's something even worse?" I couldn't downplay the sharp edge of my tone.

"If it is, we'll take care of it if it steps inside the boundaries of Mirror Lake. You have nothing to be afraid of."

Okay, maybe he didn't understand.

"I'm not afraid. I think there's more to this than what you obviously do. I think there's something supernatural at play here, and I think it's headed for Mirror Lake. We should talk to Jane. See if we can figure out what she saw. We might be able to make more sense of it than the police."

Eli frowned as his eyes narrowed on a strip of gravel between us. When he glanced at me again, I could still see the gears turning in his head.

"I'm supposed to meet my dad and some of the others tonight. I'll be sure I run this by them. I'll let you know what they say," he said.

Not the answer I was hoping for. Hopefully, someone decided I was on to something and spoke with Jane. I had a feeling there was more to what she saw than the police were giving her credit for.

4

After I left the bar, I headed back home to let Moonshine out. She licked the top of my hand as I put her harness on and hooked her up to her leash. It sucked we had to keep her locked in a cage while we were gone, but she still chewed stuff up. We couldn't leave her unsupervised for hours while we worked.

"Ready to go outside?" I asked as I started toward the front door. She darted around, tugging at the leash as though she knew what I was asking.

Once outside, we walked to her designated potty area. After she'd done her business, we started around the trailer park like usual. Moonshine enjoyed taking walks, especially when we made it to Gran's and she was able to see Winston. They were best friends.

A car crept up behind me. I stepped out of the way so they could pass.

"Hey, Mina," Taryn shouted out her rolled down

window. "That puppy is still the cutest thing I've ever seen."

"Thanks. How have you been?" I asked as she crept along beside me.

"I'm doin' okay."

"How's the baby?"

She had to be zeroing in on five months by now. Her face was plump, and the last time I saw her, she was beginning to show.

"Perfect." She grinned. "Another two weeks until we're able to find out what it is."

"Still hoping for a girl?" I asked.

"Definitely."

"Have you thought of names?"

Taryn held up a finger, asking me to give her a minute. She pulled into the driveway of her tiny trailer, cut the engine of her car, and climbed out. I walked toward her, eager to hear the names she'd come up with.

"Well, I'm still partial to Keelie," Taryn said as she popped the trunk of her car. She reached inside for a couple of plastic grocery bags. "Glenn doesn't care for it, but then again, he isn't the one growing this baby inside him. I think I should at least get to name the kid since I'm doin' all the damn work."

"Makes sense." I reached inside her trunk and grabbed the remainder of the grocery bags.

I followed her into her trailer, dragging Moonshine along with me.

"I also like Fiona and Tinley," Taryn said as she set the bags she carried inside on the tiny kitchen counter.

"At least you have a little while before you need to

decide." I placed the bags I carried on the counter beside hers and glanced around her trailer.

I'd always thought of it as a silver bullet. It was small and cute from the outside, but the inside had never seemed as homey as it did now. Taryn had spent a lot of time redecorating the inside. Glenn had landed a job at the hardware store and forced her to quit her job. He wanted her to stay home and take care of their kid. It was something she'd told me she would only agree to if she was able to redecorate.

He'd obviously stuck to her terms, and she'd done a fantastic job.

"Wow. The place looks great," I said as I picked up Moonshine and squeezed her to my chest. I didn't want her going to the bathroom on anything or chewing something up.

"Thanks. It's come a long way, but I still have a lot left to do before the baby comes." Her hand went to her belly as a wide smile graced her lips making her glow.

I didn't ask where they planned on letting the baby sleep, but I thought about it. While the place was nice, it wasn't big enough. Not for a family.

It wasn't my problem, though. They'd figure it out.

Moonshine wiggled in my arms wanting down.

"I should get going." I moved to the door. "It was nice chatting with you. And, out of the three names, I think I like Keelie best, for what it's worth."

"Thanks. Oh, did I tell you what the middle name is going to be if it's a girl?"

I shook my head. "I don't think so."

"Mina." Her eyes glistened when she spoke. "Glenn insisted, and I love the idea."

I didn't know what to say. No one had ever wanted to name their kid after me before. "Wow, thank you."

"You're welcome."

"Tell Glenn I said thank you too." I opened the door and started down the metal steps of her trailer.

"I will." Taryn beamed. "Thanks for helping with the groceries, and don't be a stranger. Glenn would love if you stopped by. Eli, too. Anytime."

"I'll let him know, thanks."

I placed Moonshine in the gravel and resumed our walk. Sunshine beat down on my face and the tops of my shoulders, but it felt good. There was a cool breeze in the air that signaled fall weather was on its way, and I was sort of sad to see the summer go.

My mind continued to circle back to Glenn and Taryn using my name as the middle name for their daughter. It was an honor, but it still left me feeling strange. I didn't understand why everyone thought me going up against Regina and her goons had been so heroic. I hadn't done anything more than the others with me that night had. Yet everyone thought I was a hero.

Truthfully, I was nothing more than a stubborn girl with an incessant need to push limits and boundaries.

"Mina!" a familiar voice called out, pulling me from my thoughts.

Mom stood in the garden with Gran. I couldn't believe Moonshine and I had already made it around the trailer park. It had taken no time at all. Usually, we were stopping every two seconds so she could sniff something. Instead, she seemed content to walk beside me and take in the scenery. She was going to be an excellent puppy to take hiking.

"Hey," I said as I stopped at the garden fence. "What are you two up to?"

"Oh, you know, just harvesting what we can and pruning off what we can't," Mom said with a smirk.

"No one is twisting your arm when it comes to helping," Gran insisted. She snipped off a few stalks of rosemary. "If you don't want to be in the garden, by all means, head back inside."

"Want to help?" Mom asked, ignoring Gran's snippy words.

I glanced at Moonshine. "No. I think I'm going to finish Moonshine's walk. She seems to be enjoying it today."

"Of course she is. It's a beautiful day," Mom said. "I wish Winston enjoyed his walks as much as she does. He only ever wants to pee on everything."

"I remember." I chuckled.

"Oh, before I forget," Gran called out. "There's a few things on the kitchen counter for you."

"Gran's been cooking." Mom wiggled her eyebrows. "She made you a couple of different herb blends and some teas."

"What for?" I asked, knowing Gran's concoctions always had a medicinal purpose.

Gran placed a hand on her hip and stopped what she'd been doing. "I had some herbs left over, so I made you an herbal first aid kit. The jars are marked. So are the pouches. There's stuff for headaches, stomach aches, a salve for cuts and burns, and so on."

"Cool. Thanks," I said.

"You're welcome. Now, go get it before you forget."

"I'll come with you," Mom said as she pulled off the gloves she'd been wearing and tossed them on the ground. "I could use a break from the sun anyway."

"Oh, poo! You haven't been out here that long," Gran insisted.

"I know, but my skin is sensitive after not having seen sunlight in so long."

Mom was only teasing, but her words still hit me in the gut. They were a reminder she'd been held prisoner too many years inside the building Regina ran.

Mom placed a hand on my shoulder and steered me toward the front door of the trailer. "She's probably sick of hearing me say that. I think I've used the same line ten times now. Gardening has never been my thing."

"It's not mine either," I said. A smile twisted the corners of my lips, another reminder of how similar we were.

"Gracie seems to enjoy it," Mom said as she started up the steps to the trailer. "If you can get her away from Cooper, that is."

I picked Moonshine up and climbed the stairs behind her. "They're still joined at the hip, huh?"

"Yup. They remind me a lot of you and Eli. There's the same sense of chemistry crackling in the air whenever they're together."

I wasn't sure how I felt about my little sister having chemistry that crackled with anyone.

"Where is Gracie now?" I stepped inside and closed the door behind me. It had been a while since I'd hung out with Gracie. I swore I'd make more time for her, but it seemed like I was never able to.

"She's school shopping with Callie and probably Cooper," Mom said in a soft tone. Sadness shifted across her face.

"She didn't want you to take her school shopping?"

"No. It's okay though. I understand. She has a life I know nothing about because she grew up without me."

Gracie had been seven when Mom disappeared. Now, she was thirteen. She had grown up without her.

"It will get better. Gracie can be stubborn some-times," I said, hoping to ease her mind.

"I know. I just keep waiting for it to happen."

"It's only been a month. Give her more time."

Mom shook her head and glanced at me. "When did you get so smart? You're so grown up." She nudged me with her shoulder.

I tucked a few stray strands of hair behind my ear. "I'm not sure."

It was a lie. I could pinpoint when I'd grown up—the moment I thought she'd left us.

"Well, this is what Gran made you," Mom said as she motioned to the jars and sashes of herbal concoctions on the kitchen counter. "Like she said, she marked them so you'll know what to use them for."

I skimmed over the labels. "This is great."

Mom reached inside the cabinet beneath the kitchen sink and pulled out a grocery bag. She placed everything inside.

"How's Dad doing?" I asked as I scratched behind Moonshine's ears.

"He's doing well. He's over at Hershel's helping him fix the potholes in his driveway."

"Has he been drinking any?" I hated to ask, but Herschel and my dad had been known to drink the day away together.

"No. He hasn't had anything since the day I came back. He swore to me he wouldn't, and so far, he's been able to keep his promise. I'm proud of him, but I worry because I know it takes a lot out of him. I know how bad of an alcoholic he was while I was gone. What he's doing can't be easy."

"I'm proud of him too."

"He's also cut back on his pill consumption. I know that makes it even more difficult for him not to turn to alcohol."

"How did you get him to do that?"

Mom flashed me a sideways smile. "It wasn't easy, but I talked him into testing a few of Gran's concoctions out for pain. He was skeptical, but he realized the gel she makes works better than a handful of pills. He also realized a lot of the pain was in his mind. A lot of it had to do with all the alcohol he was drinking, too."

"Gran always said all the alcohol he consumed was inflaming his body."

"She knows her stuff. I'm surprised he didn't listen to her."

"She does," I said.

"So, have any plans for your birthday?" An excited gleam flashed in her eyes.

"No. Not really. I'm happy with sitting around and relaxing in my PJs. I don't want anyone to make a big deal out of my birthday."

"Sorry to burst your bubble, but you know that's not going to happen, don't you?"

"A girl can dream," I said.

"No comment on if that dream will happen for you this year." Mom handed me the grocery bag full of Gran's concoctions. "I love you. I'll talk to you later. I should probably get back out to the garden, even though I don't want to."

"Better you than me." I stepped to the front door and let myself out. "Tell Gracie and Dad I said hi."

"I will."

"Love you. Talk to you later."

"Bye honey."

I headed home with a grocery bag full of herbal concoctions and Moonshine trotting beside me, trying to determine what everyone might have planned for my birthday. Were there any clues lying around the trailer? I made a note to look.

Surprises weren't my thing.

5

It was close to two in the morning when Eli came home. I'd been curled up on the couch with Moonshine watching TV for hours. I hated nights when he worked and then went to a pack meeting. I knew it was something I'd have to get used to, though. Eli was in training to become the alpha.

"Hey," he said as he kicked off his boots at the door. "I thought you'd be in bed by now."

"I wanted to wait up for you," I said as I paused the movie I'd been watching. "Did you mention anything to your dad about Jane?"

"Yeah. Apparently, he's already been in contact with Dan at the police station about her. Dan paid her a visit yesterday. He thinks she's crazy, and because of that, Dad doesn't feel there's any information we can gain from talking to her."

"What? Why?" I didn't understand how officer Dan could write her off. Of course she was crazy; she'd witnessed people being mutilated in front of her. That would be enough to drive even the sanest person crazy.

Eli's hands shot up. "I know you think she has information about the Midnight Reaper we could use to catch him, but officer Dan said she's schizophrenic or something. She never stopped looking out the window while he was talking to her. At one point, she thought spiders were crawling up her legs, but there was nothing there. She repeatedly said someone was watching her, and that she was next on his list. She's paranoid and delusional. He couldn't make sense of the things she said."

"One of us might be able to," I insisted.

"Dad thinks it's a waste of time. However, he does believe the Midnight Reaper is headed to Mirror Lake."

"Exactly what I said."

"I know. I thought you'd like that part." Eli grinned. "He wants to do patrols around town. Day and night. Which means you'll see a lot less of me until this monster is captured."

"I won't see less of you because I'm patrolling too." I lifted my chin, challenging him to argue with me.

"Figured you'd say that. I already told Dad you'd be onboard to help." Eli winked. "We're going to need all the help we can get, because, like you, Dad also believes this is something supernatural."

I was right. A chill crept up my spine. I hoped whoever was responsible would be caught before they reached Mirror Lake, but it didn't seem as though that would be possible. Hell, he'd already made it across the United States without being caught.

"Who is taking part in the patrols?" I asked.

"Dorian, Sabin, Max, Frank, Tate, Glenn, and some others. Dad suggested we ask your mom too," Eli said as he moved to sit beside me.

"I'm sure she'll want to help." I sat up straighter on the couch. Moonshine kicked her legs out as though telling me to be still. "You should ask Violet too. She might want to help."

Eli nodded. "I'll ask. The two of you could partner up during patrols."

"I'd be okay with that. Violet is a good kid." I smoothed my hand along Eli's forearm, soaking in his warmth and the feel of his coarse hair there. I'd missed him today. "I still think your dad should reconsider talking to Jane. My gut is telling me she knows something valuable."

"Your gut, huh?" Eli smirked.

I narrowed my eyes. "Are you mocking me? You should know by now never to mock my gut feelings, Eli Vargas."

"I'm not mocking you."

"Sure does seem like it."

He licked his lips and his smirk grew. "I think it's cute when you play off your intuition like that."

"It's not going to be cute when you realize I'm right."

He exhaled a slow breath. "I'm sorry, but we can't just go talk to her. My dad is really on me about doing things by the book now, especially after everything that happened last time with Drew, Peter, and Shane. All he wants me to focus on is rounding up people to patrol and setting a schedule for everyone. It isn't our job to figure out who's doing this or why. All we need is to make sure they don't get into Mirror Lake."

"I get that. I do," I said, truly meaning it.

"But?"

"No but."

"Wow, I figured you'd continue listing reasons why we should look into this further."

"Nope. I'll agree to disagree on this one for now. We'll focus on patrolling and making sure the Midnight Reaper doesn't get into town," I said. "*But.*"

Eli frowned. "And there it is."

"I do have a bone to pick with you."

"About what?"

"Oh, you know, the birthday party you're planning." I tugged on his arm hair, causing him to jerk his arm away from me. "I thought you understood I don't want a massive birthday party."

"I do," he insisted as he rubbed his arm. "I'm not throwing you a *massive* party. Only a small one. And who ratted me out?"

"Mom did," I grumbled. "It had better be small."

"Your mom? Really? I didn't think she'd be the one to do it. I figured it would be Gran, considering she was the one who found my list."

"List?"

"Well, yeah. I'm not just going to wing this. I have stuff planned. Food. Music. Drinks."

"Did Gran say something about what you have planned?" I asked.

Eli nodded. "Yup. She didn't seem happy with some of the things on my list. She scratched them out and wrote suggestions she deemed as suitable alternatives in the margins."

"Sounds like something she'd do." I laughed.

"She's not going to be happy when she sees I didn't adhere to the bulk of them."

"What did you plan that she didn't like?"

A birthday party consisted of food, beverages, and cake. Well, and music. There wasn't much Gran could disagree with.

However, this was an Eli Vargas party. Now that I thought about it, there was probably a lot she might not agree with.

"I can't tell you that. You've already ruined the surprise, or at least your mom did. You'll just have to wait until tomorrow night to find out the rest."

Tomorrow night. I couldn't believe my birthday was tomorrow. I would be turning nineteen.

Some days, I felt so much older.

"You still have the day off tomorrow from Rosemary's?"

"Yeah." I nodded. "Why? Are we doing something fun?"

"You know it. In the morning, in the afternoon, at night. Birthday booty has no limits." He winked.

"Be serious."

"I am being serious," Eli said before his lips pressed against mine.

"Fine," I muttered between kisses. "Be that way." Moonshine hopped off the couch and pranced toward the front door. She scratched at it, letting us know she needed to go outside.

"Your turn." I grinned as I pulled away from him.

"Not good timing, Moonshine, not good timing," Eli huffed as he stood to retrieve her leash.

I chuckled as I leaned back against the couch. My mind dipped to thoughts of what Eli could be planning for my birthday. Whatever it was, I had no doubt it would be fun. Now that the surprise part was out of the way, I had nothing to be pissed about. I could enjoy myself instead.

6

Fingertips toying with my panty line woke me.

"Happy birthday," Eli whispered, his hot breath tickling my ear.

"Mmmm...thank you," I muttered. My mind was still asleep, but my body was awake.

"Are you ready for your day of fun?" Eli asked as his tongue snaked out to skim along my ear.

"I guess." I still wanted to lie around in my PJs all day. Or better yet, allow Eli to spend the day worshiping my naked body.

"You'll enjoy every second. Trust me." I could hear the smile in his words.

A knock sounded at the front door, causing Eli to jerk his hand away from my most sensitive area.

"Damn. She wasn't supposed to be here for a while," he grumbled as he slipped out of bed and pulled on some clothes.

"Who wasn't supposed to be here for a while?" I asked.

"Your mom."

"What she's doing here? She didn't say anything yesterday about coming by."

"Which I find as odd as you do. She blabbed about my surprise but didn't mention hers. Imagine that," Eli grumbled. He wasn't angry, per se, but I sensed his annoyance.

"Great. You know how much I hate surprises. Why don't you just go ahead and tell me what she has planned?" I slipped out of bed.

"I'm not the type to ruin surprises." He flashed me an adorable grin before leaving the room.

I pulled on my pajama pants and listened as the front door opened. My mom's excited voice carried down the hall.

"Hey. Is Mina awake yet? Am I too early?"

"I'm awake," I said as I made my way down the hall and into the living room. "What's up?"

"Happy birthday, sweet girl!" she shouted as she rushed toward me and pulled me in for a hug.

Sweet girl. I secretly loved it when she called me that. It took me back to my childhood.

"What's with the backpack?" Goose bumps prickled across my skin because I thought I knew.

"Put on some good shoes. Whiteside Mountain is waiting." Mom winked.

My thoughts scattered. I was too excited to think. Hiking Whiteside Mountain had been a birthday tradition between my mom and me. One we'd spent years unable to do because of some filthy vampires.

"Are you serious?" I asked.

If I were being honest, a part of me thought she wouldn't remember, considering how much time had passed since our last birthday together.

"Of course." She placed a kiss on my forehead. "It used to be our thing. Are you not into hiking anymore?" Her eyebrows furrowed.

"Oh, she's into it," Eli insisted. He stepped to Moonshine's crate and let her out. "Trust me."

"I didn't think you'd want to go," I said.

"*Hello*, I was trapped inside a room held underground for six years. Of course I want to get outdoors and hike a mountain today. Anything outdoors is my jam right now." Her face became more animated, bringing a smile to my own.

"Okay, then. Let's go."

Mom chuckled. "Grab your sneakers."

I headed to the bedroom to change into appropriate hiking clothes and grab my sneakers. Afterward, I pulled my hair high on top of my head.

Eli and Mom were talking in low whispers when I entered the living room again.

"Stop that," I demanded. "No more birthday planning. Whatever's already been discussed is fine. I promise you," I said as I made my way to the kitchen to fill up a water bottle for myself.

"Don't worry about grabbing food," Mom said. "I packed enough for us both. You okay with having a picnic up there with me?"

"Yeah, sure. Sounds great." My eyes drifted to Eli. Was he not coming?

Eli stepped to where I was. His hands found their way to my hips as he pulled me close.

"I'll be here when you get back. Have fun with your mom," he insisted before placing a soft kiss to my lips.

"I will."

"Happy birthday," Eli whispered before he let me go.

I flashed him a smile and then headed to the front door. This was going to be the best birthday ever because I had my mom back, and we were keeping our Whiteside Mountain tradition.

———

"I HOPE you don't mind I dragged you out here today. I just remember how much you used to enjoy it. Figured we could recreate some old memories," Mom said as she pulled a sandwich from her backpack.

We were sitting on the same rock we used to at the highest point of the hike. It overlooked the valley. While it wasn't flat, it had grooves cut out that were the right size for my butt.

"Remember the first time we came up here?" Mom asked. She laid the rest of the food she'd brought out between us on the rock. "Your dad and Gracie came too."

"Yeah, I remember. They complained the entire time," I said before taking a bite of my sandwich. Peanut butter and honey. My favorite.

She laughed. "They did. I almost couldn't wait for

the hike to be over with so I wouldn't have to hear either of them complain anymore."

"Me too. Gracie was about in tears by the time we made it to this point. Remember?" I asked. "She dragged her feet the entire time, and complained her legs felt like they were going to fall off once we got back to the car."

"Oh, I remember. We had to take a break up here for the longest time, but it was during that break I fell in love with this place." Her gaze drifted to take in the scenery. "I sat right here and tried to calm myself down. I was so angry with both of them for ruining our hike. When you climbed up here with me and curled into my side, I knew the two of us would be back without them. You always loved the outdoors as much as I did."

The memory washed over me. The two of us had sat on this rock listening to Dad and Gracie bond in their complaining while we bonded in gazing at the beautiful sight before us.

"It was so peaceful here. One of those moments I wanted to bottle and keep forever," Mom whispered. "And then we started down the mountain again. Your dad and Gracie complained less because they knew the hike was almost over, but it still sucked to be in their presence."

"It did," I said with a nod as I took another bite of my sandwich. "Gracie started running ahead of us on the trail she was so excited we were almost to the car."

"Yup. She fell and I freaked out she'd really hurt herself."

"Oh yeah! I forgot about that," I said. "She was jumping on the rocks alongside the trail, posing like she was a statue. I remember her slipping off one. She busted her knees."

Mom nodded. "I nearly had a heart attack. I thought I saw her face bounce off the ground. I could've sworn she hit her head on the rock in front of her and when she came up I'd see blood. Thank goodness that wasn't the case."

"She was lucky."

"She was." Mom took a sip of her water. "One of her knees swelled and was black and blue for a few days. It could've been so much worse, though."

"Remember how much she milked that hurt knee afterward?" I asked with a grin.

Mom rolled her eyes. "Oh my God, yes! She went to Callie's and borrowed her dad's crutches. They were way too big for her. I thought for sure she'd break her leg by being silly with them. God, she used them for nearly two weeks."

I rolled my eyes. "She's always been such a drama queen."

"That she has." Mom glanced at me. "The two of you have always been like night and day."

"I know. We still are."

"I've noticed." She took a bite of her sandwich, but her eyes never wavered from me. "You really turned into a beautiful, strong, independent woman, Mina. I'm so proud of you."

Warmth flowed through my chest. "Thanks."

"I mean it. I'm so proud of you and who you've become." She placed a hand on my knee and gave it a gentle squeeze. "I'm sorry I couldn't be there to help guide you. It looks like you did a great job on your own, though. I love you, sweetie. Happy birthday."

"I love you too."

"I have something I want to give you. It's not much, just something I want you to have." She unzipped the front pocket of her backpack and pulled out something wrapped in white tissue paper.

"You didn't have to get me anything," I said as I took it from her. "Coming here with you was enough."

"I wanted to," she said. "This isn't everything either. Me, Gran, Gracie, and your dad all pitched in on something else. You'll get it later at Eli's–um, at home." She winked.

"At Eli's party, you mean?" I teased.

"Yes, at Eli's party." She exhaled a breath. "Sorry for spoiling that for you. I couldn't contain myself. You have no idea how many times I dreamed of being able to spend birthdays with you girls again."

"It's okay. I get it."

I reached out and pulled her into a hug. When we parted, she nodded to the gift in my hand.

"Open it."

It didn't weigh much and fit in the palm of my hand. I had no clue what it might be.

A large grin stretched across my mother's face while I tore at the tissue paper. Whatever was inside, she was pleased to be giving it to me. I peeled back the tissue paper, revealing a silver ring with a black stone.

"It's beautiful," I said. "I think I remember seeing you wear this."

"I'm sure. I used to wear it all the time. It was a gift

from my mom. Something she gave to me about a month before my parents' car accident."

"Oh. Wow." I didn't know what to say. She barely talked about her parents. I'd always imagined it was too hard for her. All I knew about them was they'd been in a bad car accident that took their lives when she was a teenager. "Thank you. I know how much this ring means to you. I promise to take care of it."

"I know you will," she said as she pulled me in for another hug. "It's been passed down from generation to generation. It was my mother's great-grandmother's. Just be sure to pass it on to one of your daughters one day. If you decide to have kids that is. I know that's probably the last thing on your mind right now."

"Uh, yeah. Kids are definitely not on my mind yet, but I promise to pass the ring on when the time comes."

"Happy birthday, honey."

"Thank you."

"All right, let's finish our lunch and head back down. I don't want to keep you too long. So many festivities are waiting for you today." Her eyes sparkled when she spoke.

"Ha ha," I said sarcastically as I slipped the ring on my middle finger and stared at it before taking another bite of my sandwich.

Best birthday present ever.

7

Eli was gone when I got home. He'd left me a sticky note on the refrigerator saying he'd be back soon and he hoped I'd enjoyed the hike with my mom. I left the sticky note on the fridge and headed to Moonshine's crate.

After taking her out, I gathered some clean clothes and headed to the bathroom for a shower.

Lukewarm water slipped over my skin as I thought about how different this birthday was compared to my last. In the course of a few months, my entire life had completed a one-eighty. Eli and I were imprinted and bonded in a way that was hard to put into words. Mom was back in my life, safe and sound. Dad was sober for the first time in years. I had a job and was in college. I'd moved out of Gran's.

Best of all, I was happy. Truly happy.

A new text came through on my cell, pulling me from my thoughts. I finished rinsing my hair, eager to see if it was Eli. The anticipation of what he had in store for me today had me on pins and needles.

I shut the water off and grabbed a towel before reaching for my phone. The text wasn't from Eli. It was from Ridley.

Happy birthday! I know you have a busy day planned, but I thought maybe you'd want to meet for coffee?

Warmth centered in my chest. I loved I had people in my life who wanted to wish me happy birthday. For a split second, my mind dipped back to the email I'd gotten a week earlier from Alec. He'd been embarrassed for getting the date of my birthday wrong, but I was touched he'd cared enough to remember.

Thanks! And absolutely! Where do you want to go? — Mina

Eli could wait on me if he came back while I was gone. Besides, I hadn't been able to spend much time with Ridley the last few weeks. The bulk of my time had been spent at work or school, and before that it was spent with my family or Eli. While I wasn't much for coffee, I could go for a green tea frappe.

Shouldn't you be the one to decide where we go? After all, it is your birthday.

Okay. How about that place on Main Street? — Mina

I towel dried my hair while I waited for her to respond.

Sounds good. When do you want to meet?

Is thirty minutes okay? — Mina

Sure! See you soon.

———

WHILE MIRROR LAKE WAS SMALL, Main Street was always busy. Shops and restaurants lined both sides of the double-lane street, making it hard to find a parking space in front of the coffee shop. I didn't mind walking though. The fresh air was nice.

I spotted Ridley on the metal bench outside Hava Cup Bistro. She was smiling at her cell.

Was she texting Benji?

I loved the two of them as a couple. Their relationship was cuter than ever.

"Hey," I called out as I neared her. "How long have you been waiting?"

"Oh, hey! Not long." Ridley stood and tucked her phone away. "How's your birthday been so far?"

"It's been great," I said, unable to suppress the wide smile that spread across my face. "My mom took me to Whiteside Mountain for a hike this morning. It was something we used to do before." I didn't have to elaborate, Ridley knew the rest of that story. "It was sort of our tradition. We hiked it two birthdays in a row."

"Oh, that sounds like fun! I'm glad she's back, and that you were able to do that with her again," Ridley said as she opened the door to the coffee shop and stepped inside.

The scent of freshly brewed coffee rushed to my nose as the sounds of the place floated to my ears.

"Thanks. Me too."

We stepped in line behind a group of teenage girls. The shortest was chatting animatedly about some guy named Dylan. Apparently, he'd dumped her the night before. From the way her friend on the right glared at her, it was clear this wasn't a surprise.

"Do you and Eli have plans later?" Ridley asked, pulling my attention to her.

"Something is planned; I'm just not sure what. I know there's a surprise party, but other than that, I don't know."

Did she know something? Would Eli have come to her for ideas? My gaze skimmed over her profile.

"Sounds fun," she said.

I shrugged. "I guess. I'm not one for surprise parties."

"How can it be a surprise if you already know about it?" she teased.

"True," I said as we moved up in line. "Who were you texting? Benji?"

"Yeah." Her face lit up. "He said happy birthday, by the way."

"Tell him I said thanks."

"Have you talked with anyone else today?" Ridley asked over the loud noise of the coffee grinder.

"Becca sent me a text earlier, and Alec wished me happy birthday last week via email."

She arched a brow. "Last week?"

"He got his days mixed up."

"Okay, so why did he email instead of texting or calling? That seems weird. Who uses email anymore?"

"Apparently, he lost his phone and wanted to make

sure he didn't miss wishing me a happy birthday. He didn't realize he was a week early. I felt bad pointing it out, but it was still pretty funny. He was super embarrassed."

"I bet. Poor guy." She stepped closer to me, letting an older couple leaving a table have more room to get by. "How's everything else been? Things still going okay with living with Eli?"

"Yeah. For the most part. I mean, we've had a couple of arguments about where to put things, but other than that it's been good. I like living with him."

I didn't just *like* living with him, I *loved* it.

"That's awesome," Ridley said as we moved up in line. "Where is he? Is he working, or does he have the day off?"

"I'm not sure where he's at to be honest. He's probably out getting stuff for my surprise party." I laughed. "When I came back from my hike there was a note on the fridge saying he'd be back later."

"I'm sure whatever he's got planned is going to be spectacular."

"Maybe."

The teenage girls in front of us placed their orders and then stepped aside to wait. The shorter one was still going on about her break up. From the look on her friends' faces, they seemed sick of hearing about it. Heck, even I was tired of hearing it, and I didn't know the girl.

"Hey. What can I get for you today?" the blond barista with a pixie cut asked us.

I ordered my usual green tea frappe while Ridley ordered a salted caramel latte. She paid for both drinks before I could pull out my wallet. I thanked her as we stepped to the side.

"So, how have things been at the inn?" I asked after we situated ourselves at a table.

"Pretty good. Busy, but good. The closer it gets to fall, the more guests we have," she said as she pulled the lid off her latte and set it aside. "I don't mind, though. I like it when the house is full. The energy from all the people is pretty cool."

"How's everything else?" I asked as I motioned to all of her, hoping she understood I was asking about her magic.

She was a Caraway witch. They were known as the most powerful witches in Mirror Lake. In Ridley's case though, she didn't harbor much magic. Gran had once said she might be a late bloomer like I was when it came to becoming moon kissed. While I wasn't sure if that was the case with Ridley, I did know what it felt like to feel different. Especially when compared to the others in your family.

"Nothing new to report there. I get vibes sometimes about places or objects. It's generally stronger if it's a place or an object attached to someone who's passed away, but that's about it. Nothing spectacular. My aunt has been working with me, but nothing seems to trigger my magic." She adjusted her glasses and allowed her gaze to drift to the latte clasped between her hands giving me the impression the topic wasn't one she was comfortable discussing. "I'm okay with it. I mean, I guess. If all I can do is get vibes off things, then that's all I can do, right? At least it's something." She shrugged.

She was lying. She wasn't okay with that being all she could do. Who would be when you came from a legendary family of witches like she did?

Ridley wanted something more, and I hoped one day she'd get it. She deserved to be as powerful as her aunt and cousins.

"Oh, before I forget. I have something for you," she said as she twisted to reach inside her purse. She pulled out a box the size of my phone wrapped in sparkly green paper. "It's not much."

"You didn't have to get me anything. Meeting here and hanging out was enough," I said, meaning every word.

"I wanted to. Happy birthday."

I took it from her and carefully tore off the paper. Inside the box was a silver keychain that said *the forest calls and I must go.*

"I love it!"

"I'm glad. I saw it the other day and thought of you."

"It's so cute. Thanks."

A text came through on my cell. I reached for my phone. It was Eli.

Are you still at the coffee shop with Ridley?

"Is it Eli?" Ridley asked as she sipped her latte.

I nodded. "He must be back at our place. He's asking if I'm still here with you."

"We can go if you need to."

"No, it's okay. We can hang out for a little while longer. He won't mind," I said as I sent him a reply letting him know I was still with her and would be home soon.

He texted me right back.

Enjoy.

"You two are so cute together," Ridley insisted.

"Thanks." My cheeks grew warm. I set my phone down and took a sip from my drink. "So, do you like all your classes? I figured we'd have at least one together, but I guess not."

"I know. I can't believe that either. I figured we'd at least see each other on campus. It's not like it's gigantic." She laughed. "But, yeah. I guess I enjoy my classes so far. What about you?"

"Yeah, I like them." A guy at the bistro table behind me bumped my chair when he scooted his out to stand. I flashed him a dirty look when he didn't apologize, and then shifted my attention back to Ridley. "I think it's going to be hard managing work and school, though. It's not something I've had to deal with before."

Ridley waved my words away. "You'll find a balance that works for you after a couple of weeks. Trust me."

She knew what she was talking about. During high school she'd worked at her aunt's inn.

"I hope so," I said.

My stomach knotted as the conversation from a table behind us floated to my ears.

"I heard there was another body found this morning," the younger woman said. "Apparently, it was a thirty-two-year-old woman found while some guy was jogging. Could you imagine? I mean, I don't know what I'd do if I was jogging along, minding my own business, and came across something like that. They said the body was mutilated like the other victims of the Midnight Reaper."

"That's awful!" another woman said. "Where was this one?"

"That's the worst part. It was only about thirty miles outside of town."

The other woman gasped. "That's too close for comfort! When are they going to catch whoever this is?"

"My thoughts exactly. I told you the killer was going to make his way here. I had one of my feelings about it right after they reported about the last two women."

"I don't like this at all," the other woman said.

"Me neither. Leah is pissed because I haven't let her go out with her friends much since they reported about those two women in the city being murdered. Now, I don't think I'll let her go out at all—especially not after dark—until this person is caught."

"I don't blame you. I'll probably do the same for the boys. Actually, I wish the town would create a mandatory curfew. Then maybe it wouldn't seem as though we were torturing our teenagers."

"You know they'd think we were torturing them regardless," the first woman cackled.

"True," the second woman said.

I bit my bottom lip. My eyes locked with Ridley's across the table. It was clear from the look on her face she'd been eavesdropping on the two women behind me as well. They were talking loud enough for nearly everyone in the coffee shop to overhear their conversation.

"Do you think it's something supernatural?" Ridley whispered.

I nodded. "Do you?"

"Yeah."

"What are you thinking it is?" I asked.

She leaned in closer. "I'm not sure. A vampire maybe? I heard some of the bodies were drained of blood."

"Where did you hear that?"

I thought about the news articles I'd read and the reports I'd heard. None of them mentioned anyone being drained of blood.

"I overheard my aunt talking to a friend of hers who lives in the city. She said the women they found the other day, the ones that were on the news yesterday, had been drained of blood and mutilated."

My stomach churned.

"Who did she hear that from? I don't remember it being mentioned on the news."

Ridley took another sip of her latte. "Her husband is on the police force. He's also a witch, so he knows of the supernatural world."

Shit. The Midnight Reaper definitely sounded like a vampire now.

"Did she let our alpha know?" I asked. Weren't they supposed to keep each other in the loop? It seemed like something they should do in this situation.

"Not yet. She's supposed to talk to him later this afternoon."

Would he decide to speak with Jane afterward? I couldn't help but wonder.

"Did you hear about that girl, Jane Hawker?" I asked.

She shook her head. "No. What about her?"

"She was in the city when those two women were

attacked and witnessed the whole thing. Apparently, she's gone nuts since. She won't leave her room, and she keeps staring out the window, claiming a monster is going to get her."

"That's horrible! Has anyone from your pack spoke with her yet?"

"No. I mentioned something to Eli about it, and he said something to his dad, but the alpha doesn't see a point in talking to her. He doesn't think she can tell us anything of use. Thinks her mind is too fragile, I guess." I nodded over my shoulder to the women behind me. "I think they were right to be concerned about the killer coming here."

"Me too," Ridley insisted. "Is your pack making any preparations to try and stop this person once he gets into Mirror Lake? My aunt was contemplating putting a ward up. One that would keep any vampires besides the Montevallos out of town now that she suspects the Midnight Reaper is a vampire. She's already been gathering ingredients."

"That's a good idea. We're running patrols. Hopefully this guy will be caught soon. I don't want a vampire serial killer walking our streets and lurking in our woods." The thought sent a shiver up my spine.

"I don't think any of us do."

"Are the Montevallos doing anything to help?" I asked before taking another sip from my frappe.

"I'm not sure, but there are three of them in town now."

Three? I only knew of two.

"I've met Julian and his younger sister, Ivette, but I

haven't met anyone else. Who's the other?" My curiosity was piqued.

"Her name is Octavia. I think she's older than Julian and Ivette."

"Oh, well regardless of age and stuff, I think they should help. This Midnight Reaper isn't going to be any kinder to our tiny town or its residents than it has been elsewhere."

Maybe I would pay the Montevallos a visit and say so.

8

Eli stood in the kitchen, refilling Moonshine's water bowl when I walked in.

"Hey," he called from over his shoulder. "How was coffee with Ridley?"

Moonshine ignored the fact Eli had filled her bowl and darted to me. She jumped up, excited to see me.

"Good," I said as I bent down to pet her. "Until I overheard a conversation at the table behind us. There were these two women talking about the Midnight Reaper. Did you know another body was found? Thirty miles from here?" I asked as I glanced at him.

His body stiffened. "Yeah. Dad mentioned it earlier."

"Why didn't you say anything?" I snapped.

"Because it's your birthday," he said as though this should be reason enough. "It's supposed to be a happy day. I didn't want you thinking about the killings or the Midnight Reaper all day."

I wanted to be mad at him, but I understood where

he was coming from. Still, I couldn't drop the subject. This was serious, and it was starting to freak me out.

"Did you know the bodies weren't just mutilated, they were drained of blood too?" The words rushed from my lips. "It's a vampire doing all of this."

"Where did you hear that?"

Tightness built in my chest as I cocked my head to the side, studying his expression. I licked my lips as I continued to scratch Moonshine behind the ear.

"Did you know?" I asked.

Eli exhaled a slow breath. "It's been speculated, but Dad hasn't given a definite answer to any of us yet. We've all thought it may be something supernatural responsible though. Humans don't mutilate others like that."

"Why would he withhold information like that from you guys?"

Eli shrugged. "Maybe he needs more evidence?" He leaned against the kitchen counter and folded his arms over his chest. His green eyes narrowed on me. "Who did you hear all this from? Was it a legitimate source?"

"Ridley mentioned it." I stepped away from Moonshine to lean against the kitchen counter as well. "Her aunt heard about it from a friend of hers who lives in the city. She and her husband are witches. He's also on the police force. He told her some of the bodies were drained of blood as well as mutilated."

Eli rubbed his jaw, his mind working overtime. "So what does that mean? Is this one vampire we're dealing with or two?"

My heart lodged in my throat. I hadn't thought of the Midnight Reaper as more than one person.

There was a real chance this wasn't a single supernatural being we were talking about but multiple beings.

"It could be more than one supernatural creature too. A vampire and something else." I scooped up Moonshine as she lapped at her water, and I hugged her to my chest. I needed comfort, and she was a pro at giving it. "I still think we need to talk to Jane Hawker. So far she's the only person who has witnessed whatever it is we're dealing with."

"She's gone crazy, Mina. I'm not sure we'll be able to get much information out of her."

"We have to try."

"I'll talk to my dad again and see what he suggests," Eli said. "But not until after your party."

"Talk to him now," I insisted.

"No." His eyes grew dark. He was serious, but so was I. "We're going to your party, and we're going to enjoy ourselves. All of this can wait until after."

"Can it? Whatever is out there is probably on its way to town as we speak. The Caraways are doing something about it. Why shouldn't we? Mirror Lake is our home too. We need to help protect it."

"What are the witches doing?"

"Ridley said they're gathering ingredients to set a ward in place that won't allow any vampires except the Montevallos in town."

"That's a good idea," Eli said. "And we are doing something. We're patrolling. Your shift is tomorrow night. You and Violet were placed together."

"Good," I said. It was a start.

"Dad is supposed to meet with the Montevallos tomorrow. Ridley's aunt too."

"Maybe between the three of us we can keep the Midnight Reaper out of Mirror Lake." My voice shook when I spoke. I wanted to believe what I'd said, but had an awful feeling twisting in the pit of my stomach.

One that had me thinking something horrible would happen soon.

I set Moonshine down when she wiggled in my arms. Could she feel the tension and worry creeping through my veins? They say animals can sense things of that nature; I knew my wolf could. I could feel her pacing inside me. Anxious. Tense. On edge. Exactly like me.

"Hey." Eli lifted my chin, forcing me to look at him. "Chin up. It's your birthday. Don't worry about all of this crap now."

I frowned. "Easier said than done."

"Let me take your mind off it then," he said as he bent to press his lips against mine.

Lust clouded my thoughts as I gave in to him. His lips. His touch. His warmth. His arms snaked around my waist, pulling me closer as he skimmed his tongue over my bottom lip wanting to deepen our kiss. I opened my mouth and brushed my tongue against his, wanting him to make me forget the real possibility of all hell about to break loose in Mirror Lake yet again.

Eli's tongue tangled with mine as he did as I wanted. His fingertips dug into the flesh of my hips. I ran my fingers through the hair at the nape of his neck. A groan spurred from somewhere deep inside his chest as I grazed my teeth across his bottom lip.

We made our way out of the kitchen and through the living room toward our bedroom. Once we reached the hall, something soft fluttered past me, touching my leg in the process.

"What the?" Eli pulled away as we became tangled in something.

Toilet paper. It trailed down the hall from the bathroom toward the living room.

"Moonshine must've gotten into the bathroom somehow," Eli growled.

She must have heard her name because the toilet paper began moving again as a low growling noise filled the trailer.

I followed Eli to the living room where I spotted Moonshine racing around the couch with toilet paper flying behind her. Eli bolted after her as I laughed, watching the two of them circle the couch.

"Help me. Don't just stand there," Eli snapped.

I headed in the opposite direction Moonshine was going, hoping to block her path and trap her. It worked. With no place to go, she paused long enough for Eli to grab her. He ripped a long piece of toilet paper from her mouth, and then pried her lips apart with his fingers to dig out the rest.

"I'm pretty sure she swallowed some," he muttered.

I scooped up the toilet paper and tossed it in the trash. "It's just paper. She should be okay."

Eli blew out a long breath and set her down. "It seems like every time we get started, something comes along and grinds it to a halt."

"I know." I walked toward him, thinking it would be

easy to pick up where we'd left off. "So let's not give anyone an excuse to interrupt us." I placed a quick kiss on his lips before heading to the front door to lock it. Next, I gathered our cell phones and turned them off before I put Moonshine in her crate.

"I like the way you think." Eli grinned.

I sauntered toward him and grabbed at the front of his shirt. I headed toward our bedroom, pulling him along with me. He didn't fight. In fact, he seemed to like me showing a little dominance.

Once we reached the bedroom, I released my grip on him and peeled off my clothes. I was going to get some birthday booty, damn it.

"A little eager, aren't you?"

I tossed my shirt to the floor. "Always."

"Hmm...I like the sound of that," Eli said as he stripped and flopped onto the bed.

A grin hung on my face as I moved to straddle him. I placed warm kisses along the side of his neck and allowed myself to become lost in him again. His fingertips dug into my hips as a low growl pushed its way past his lips. I closed my eyes as I continued to kiss his beautiful skin.

This was what I'd wanted for my birthday—some alone time with Eli.

9

Butterflies burst through my stomach as I pulled my hair on top of my head. I'd never been more nervous to attend a party in my life. I knew this one only consisted of pack members, but I still couldn't tame my anxiety.

"Are you ready?" Eli asked. He stood in the bedroom doorway, watching me fret with my hair.

I exhaled a long breath, puffing out my cheeks. "As ready as I'll ever be."

"Don't look so depressed and ill. It's a party. For you. You're supposed to be happy," Eli insisted with a teasing grin.

"I am happy. I'm just nervous."

"Why would you be nervous?" He chuckled.

"I just am." I shrugged.

My hands dropped to my sides as I walked past him into the hall.

"Well, don't be. I planned a fun party. Lots of food.

Good music," Eli said as he followed me down the hall. "Hell, I even bought some moonshine for us to sneak a drink of. That's what your Gran saw on my list and didn't seem happy about."

I glared at him over my shoulder. Drinking around my dad didn't seem right. Not after he'd been working so hard to stay sober.

"I don't think drinking alcohol tonight is a good idea." I faced him once we reached the living room. "I know this is a party, and I know it's not realistic to think my dad will never be around alcohol again, but I do think it's too soon. He doesn't need any temptation, and I don't want everyone to act like he's an elephant in the room they need to avoid either."

Eli scratched the back of his neck. "I'm sorry. I should've thought the whole alcohol thing through better. I won't bring it."

"Thanks," I said as I leaned in and placed a kiss on his cheek. "So, the question is: Are you ready?"

I hated putting him on the spot, but not serving alcohol was for the best.

"Actually," he said as he sidestepped me. He headed toward the washer and dryer. "I have something for you."

"A new washer and dryer?" I scrunched up my face. "Because really, you didn't have to. The set we have is fine. There's no washer or dryer you could get that would make doing laundry fun."

"No. Not a new washer or dryer." He rummaged around before grabbing something he shoved behind his back. "Something even better."

"What?" I asked as I tried to peer around him to see what he was holding. I couldn't.

"Paint." He held a gallon out to me, along with a stir stick. "Purple paint. Professor Plum to be exact."

My jaw dropped. "You're kidding! You bought me paint? Purple paint? Oh my God!"

And here I'd thought this birthday couldn't get any better.

"That was part of our bet. You did win, remember?" He grinned and I had to kiss him.

"I do remember," I said between kisses. "This is the best. Thank you!"

"You're welcome." He set the paint on the kitchen counter and pried the lid off with a flathead screwdriver from in the junk drawer. "Check the color out. See if you like it."

The scent of wet paint floated through the air as the lid came off, and I found myself smiling wide. I loved painting. There was nothing better than changing the color of your walls to switch up the entire feel of a space.

Eli dipped the stir stick into the thick paint and swirled it around.

"It's a little darker than I thought it would be," he said, sounding slightly afraid.

"Don't be scared. It will dry lighter I'm sure."

I lifted the lid off the counter and grabbed a paint-brush from under the kitchen sink, then headed to our room. My muscles tingled and my mind felt clearer as I swiped a few strokes of color onto the wall. When I was finished, I took a step back and stared.

"It's going to look beautiful," I said. My gaze drifted to Eli. "Do you like it?"

"Umm, yeah. Sure." He scratched at his neck.

My arm fell to my side. "You hate it."

"I don't hate it. I just think it will take some getting used to."

He hated it. Disappointment crashed through me. I didn't want to paint the walls a color he loathed.

"It's fine. I'm sure it will grow on me," he said as he pulled me close. "I don't care what color the walls are. All I care about is waking up next to you every day."

He was too sweet to me sometimes.

"Let's get out of here," Eli said as he took the paint lid from me. "You have a party to get to."

I followed him down the hall. "That needs to dry anyway. Maybe you'll like it then."

He chuckled as he placed the lid back on the can. I moved to the pantry and grabbed a plastic grocery bag to wrap the wet brush in.

"Ready?" Eli asked.

"Yeah." I pointed to Moonshine who was following him toward the front door. "Are we not putting her up this time?"

"I figured I'd pop back in to check on her in about an hour. There isn't anything she can get into. I've already made sure."

"Why don't we take her with us," I suggested. "Gracie will probably bring Winston. They can have a puppy playdate."

"Okay, sure. Grab her leash."

I grabbed it off the counter and started for the door.

Once we had her hooked up, the three of us stepped outside.

It was close to seven, which meant it was cooling off and the sky was beginning to darken. I enjoyed this time of year.

I walked beside Eli down the gravel road to the back of the trailer park. There was no central section designated for parties. Instead, Eli's dad had asked the trailer park owner for a small building near the back.

Bobby had no issue with putting one up. He was a good guy.

Once the building was built we put it to use. Throughout the year we hosted multiple events there—ceremonial dinners, potlucks, birthday parties, and holidays. The space had brought us closer as a pack through the functions we held.

Music floated to my ears as we neared it. Someone had hung a string of white lights around the door and tiny windows, causing it to stand out against the beautiful sky. Kids played out front while a few of the adult pack members watched them and chatted. One of the kids held Winston in her arms. My gaze drifted around because I knew Gracie had to be close by. I spotted her leaning up against the building, watching while she chatted with Cooper.

I nodded toward them. "The two of them are inseparable lately."

"They've been close for a while," Eli insisted.

"Do you think they're going to imprint once they become moon kissed?" I asked, unable to take my eyes off them.

It was hard for me to think of Gracie in such a grown-up way, but she would be turning fourteen soon. She was growing up whether I wanted her to or not.

"It's possible." Eli grinned. Excitement rang in his voice.

"Ugh," I said as I smoothed a hand over my face. "I can't believe I'm talking about my little sister becoming imprinted."

"It's bound to happen one day."

"I know. It's just crazy to see her with someone and think about it. I mean, she has a boyfriend! One she's been with for two months. It's insane!"

"It's normal," Eli insisted.

"Look! They brought Moonshine!" one of Sylvie's girls shouted. She ran to where we were, almost smacking into Eli. "Can I hold her? Please! I won't let her go. I promise."

Eli glanced at me. I shrugged and flashed him a smile.

"Okay, sure. Just be careful she doesn't get off this leash. She's a hard one to catch," Eli said.

"Trust him," I said. "He had a hard time catching her this afternoon when she got a hold of some toilet paper." I grinned, remembering the entire fiasco.

"Toilet paper? Ew, gross!" She made a disgusted face.

"It wasn't used," Eli said.

She reached out for the leash and ran away with her, ignoring Eli. Other kids came running up eager to pet her. She was the star for a moment while they greeted her, and she licked their tiny fingers.

Eli stepped in front of me, blocking my view.

"Stay here for a minute," he insisted.

"Why? Are you going to warn the others I'm here?" I teased.

"I am."

"Don't you think that's a little pointless since I already know about the party?"

"No. Stay right here," he insisted once more as he walked away from me backward to the door of the building.

I folded my arms over my chest and rolled my eyes but remained where I was.

"Hey! Happy birthday," Gracie said as she walked to where I stood. Cooper followed her like a puppy.

I pulled her in for a hug. "Thanks."

Had she gotten taller since the last time I saw her?

"Have you had a good birthday so far?" she asked once we released each other.

I nodded. "Oh, yeah."

"Mom said she took you to Whiteside Mountain."

"She did. It was nice to be back there with her again."

"I bet."

We lapsed into an awkward silence. When had it become so difficult to talk to my little sister?

"Well, I'm glad your birthday has been a good one so far. We're going to slip inside," she said as she nodded toward the building. "I guess we're going to yell surprise with everyone else. Even though I don't see the point since you're already here and know there's a party happening for your birthday." She chuckled as she rolled her eyes.

"I'll be here. Waiting to pretend to be surprised."

"It's the thought that counts." Cooper winked as they walked away.

He was cute. I'd give him that. He shared Eli's eyes, same dark hair, and some facial features. I could see why Gracie was smitten with him. Something about those Vargas boys got under your skin in the best of ways. I knew the feeling well.

Time moved slowly as I waited for Eli to come back. I watched the kids play with Winston and Moonshine. I wasn't sure who was having more fun—the puppies or them.

"Ready for this?" Eli asked from behind me. I tucked a few stray strands of hair behind my ear.

"Yeah. Let's do this."

My heart rate picked up. I hated this. Being the center of attention had never been something I was comfortable with.

Eli held out a hand. His face lit up when I placed mine inside it. "Close your eyes."

I inhaled a deep breath, and then exhaled as I did as he asked. He gripped my waist with his free hand, and steered me inside the building. The music was turned down, but it still played in the background. The scent of something sweet lingered in the air. It was warmer inside by a few degrees, and I thought it was because of the people crammed inside. I could feel their presence, feel their eyes on me. My cheeks heated under their stare.

Once Eli had me where he wanted, he leaned in and whispered, "You can look now."

I licked my lips and inhaled a deep breath before opening my eyes.

Ridley, Benji, Becca, and Alec stood in front of me surrounded by my pack.

A chorus of surprise rang out, but all I could focus on were my friends. How were they here? How had I not known they would be? Whose idea was it to ask them to come?

Ridley hadn't given any indication earlier she'd be here tonight. Neither had Becca when I talked to her earlier, or Alec when he sent me a text.

"Are you surprised?" Eli asked. He wrapped his arms around my waist from behind and pulled me against his chest to place a kiss on the crown of my head. "You seem surprised."

"I'm definitely surprised."

"What are you guys doing here? How?" My words were rushed and frantic sounding even to my own ears.

"We couldn't miss your birthday," Alec said.

Becca nodded. "You only turn nineteen once."

I untangled myself from Eli and pulled Becca in for a hug. Coming back to Mirror Lake had to have been difficult for her. She'd left for college shortly after Shane passed. Culinary school had probably been one of the best things to happen to her because it meant she got to put distance between herself and painful memories. I was touched she was here tonight.

"Thanks for coming," I said. "I'm so glad you're here."

"I wouldn't miss it," Becca said.

My attention drifted to Ridley next.

"You," I said with mock anger. "How could you not

say anything about this? You even asked if I'd heard from Becca or Alec today."

"I should go into acting." Her cheeks turned pink as she adjusted her glasses.

"You should because you really had me fooled." I pulled her in for a hug too.

"She really should," Benji said as he stepped forward for a hug. "She acts with me all the time."

"Is that so?" Eli asked, insinuating something different from what Benji meant.

Benji's face grew tomato red. "I didn't mean it like that!"

"Of course you didn't." Eli smirked. I jabbed him in the side with my elbow, and he let out a grunt.

After I said hello to Alec and Benji someone turned the music up again.

Eli's arm slipped around my waist as he fused himself to my side. "Happy birthday." He grinned.

"Thank you." I smiled at him. "This is been the best birthday ever. Seriously."

"Excuse me," Gran insisted as she pushed her way through the crowd. "I need to wish my granddaughter a happy birthday. I haven't seen her all day."

Flickers of guilt shifted through me. Birthdays had always been a special occurrence in the Ryan household. The day started with being woken by Gran before the sun came up. She always held a cupcake in her hand with a single lit candle. A soft rendition of happy birthday would be sung before you were allowed to blow out your candle. Next, you'd be prompted to get out of bed and head outside with her. There she'd make you circle the trailer at her side until you found the best view of the moon. Meditation and a mental reflection of your previous year would have to happen before you were allowed inside again. A large breakfast consisting of your favorite foods, a million hugs and kisses, and a small gift came next.

How had all of this slipped my mind? My heart ached for having forgotten.

"Did you do your meditation and reflection this morning?" Gran asked as she arched an eyebrow at me. It was clear she already knew I hadn't.

"No." I swallowed hard, waiting for her to reprimand me.

"I didn't think so."

"I'll do it tonight. I promise."

Gran placed a hand on my shoulder. "You don't have to. I've just always thought it was a nice way to begin a birthday."

I opened my mouth to say something, to agree, but my mom and dad walked up to me next.

"Mina! Happy birthday, sweet girl!" Mom shouted. She pulled me into a hug. Dad stood behind her, waiting for his turn. "I'm so glad we got to go on a hike today."

"Me too," I said as my gaze drifted back to Gran.

I'd hurt her, and I hated myself for it.

"Happy birthday, honey," Dad said as he pulled me in for a hug of his own.

"Thanks."

The words to happy birthday echoed through the tiny building as Eli's mom carried a cake toward me. The top was ablaze with candles, making it look like a fire hazard.

"Look at all those candles," Eli said. "Damn, you're getting old."

"Still not as old as you," I insisted.

"Somehow, I doubt you'll ever catch up."

I chuckled as his mom paused in front of me with the cake.

"Make a wish," she said.

I closed my eyes and thought long and hard in an effort to form a good wish. Before I could decide on something, a loud scream came from somewhere outside. It was followed by the puppies barking and others yelling.

All hell had broken loose outside, and I was afraid to see what had caused it.

10

Another scream echoed through the building. It was less shrill and sharp than before. Whoever had screamed was growing weaker by the second.

I blew out my candles without making a wish and raced to the door behind everyone else. My feet faltered when I saw who had screamed. A girl. Dressed in a white nightgown. She stumbled toward us. Her long black hair fell to her waist in a disheveled mess. Mascara was smudged beneath her eyes, and her skin appeared slick with sweat and ashen. Her plump lips formed the shape of an O as though she were struggling to scream but unable to make a sound.

My heart hammered hard and fast inside my chest, not because of her presence or the eeriness emanating from her looks but because of the blood soaking the neckline of her nightgown.

I didn't have to step closer to her to know I'd find two

puncture marks on her throat. I also didn't have to guess any longer if the Midnight Reaper would make his way to Mirror Lake.

Standing there, I already knew the answer to both questions, and it was enough to send my mind racing as fast as my heart. The Midnight Reaper was here, and this was one of his victims.

Happy freaking birthday to me.

"Get the kids inside!" our alpha shouted. He jumped into action while the bulk of us stared at the girl. "Charles, make sure everyone gets inside safely. Frank, Sabin, and Glenn, you're heading out with me. We need to find who did this. There's a chance he might still be around. Dorian call nine-one-one. Eli, I want you to call Officer Dan. Give him a heads up. Tate, help Charles get everyone inside and secure the building."

Everyone jumped into action, following the alpha's orders. I spotted Dorian on his phone as he rushed to the girl's side. Eli was beside him, chatting with Officer Dan. The girl made a noise, drawing my attention back to her. She didn't look well.

A loud scream bellowed past her lips. Goose bumps prickled across my skin.

"Get them off me!" she shouted. She smacked at her body as though she saw something I didn't.

Oh, shit. Was this girl Jane Hawker?

Hadn't I heard someone say she kept claiming spiders were crawling on her when no one else could see them?

Her being here, bleeding from her neck and acting the way she was, was proof enough to me the Midnight Reaper was close. I sought Ridley. If the Midnight

Reaper had made its way to Mirror Lake, it meant her family hadn't put their ward in place yet.

Ridley stood with Alec, Benji, and Becca. Her eyes widened when she caught sight of me, and she nodded toward them. I knew what she was trying to convey. This was supernatural related, and they were human.

I hoped everyone remembered my human friends were among us tonight, and no one decided to shift. I didn't know what implications it might have on Alec's brain after he'd been compelled to forget once about the supernatural world. Would it jog the year's worth of memories he'd been forced to forget?

I rushed to Ridley.

"I take it your aunt didn't have time to put the ward up yet?" I asked in a whisper.

Ridley shook her head. "Not yet, no."

"Crap," I muttered.

I glanced to the woods. The girl couldn't have walked far in her condition, which meant the alpha was right in thinking the one responsible was nearby. The kids had already been ushered inside the party building, as well as some of the other pack members, but my friends still stood out in the open with me. My gaze drifted over each of them, taking in their expressions. Benji's face had grown pale, making him appear as though he were at risk of passing out any second. Becca looked worried. Her body seemed tense as though she were ready to fight or run. And Alec, he'd stepped forward a few feet. His determination to help the girl vibrated in the air around him.

I reached out for him. "Don't. You can't help her."

"I know CPR. There might be something I can do," he insisted without making eye contact with me. He was fixated on the girl, waiting for the word to jump into action.

"Dorian is on the phone with the nine-one-one operator. I'm sure she's telling him everything he needs to know in order to help her."

Alec's fists balled at his sides. "I feel like I should do something. There's so much blood. What did this to her?" he asked.

How could I explain without mentioning vampires?

"An animal. One that could still be lurking around here somewhere. We should probably head inside with the others," Ridley insisted.

Thank you, I mouthed. I was glad she'd said something because I couldn't think of a justifiable answer, considering I was having as hard a time as Alec staying put.

"I think I'm gonna be sick," Benji muttered. He dashed to the nearest trash can. Ridley rushed to him and smoothed a hand over his back. "It's too much blood. Why is there so much blood?" he asked.

"I'm not sure, but everything will be okay," Ridley insisted.

There was a tremor in her words. An uncertainty.

I felt it too.

Regardless of what she'd said, nothing would be okay. Not after this moment. The harsh reality was that the supernatural world had touched my human friends again, and I was the person responsible for it. They'd all been here because of me. It was my birthday they were here to celebrate.

My stomach twisted at the thought.

Eli stepped to where I was. "Come here for a second." He interlaced to his fingers through mine and pulled me away from the others.

He walked me toward the girl, pausing only once we were about two feet away. The coppery scent of her blood hung heavy in the air, souring my stomach. My gaze fixed on her.

Was she breathing? Dorian blocked my view. I couldn't tell if her chest was rising or falling. I couldn't see if her eyes were open. He was hunched over her, his phone still pressed against his ear as he chatted with the nine-one-one operator.

Sirens sounded in the distance, but I knew they were still minutes away.

"Is she okay?" I asked, meaning *is she still alive.*

"No," Eli said. My heart stopped as my gaze swung to look at him. He smoothed a hand along the back of his neck. "She's...dead."

Dead. The word lingered between us, siphoning all the breath from my lungs and forcing a shiver to slip along my spine. My gaze drifted back to what little I could see of her. Sadness crept through me, numbing my fear.

"Who was she? Was it Jane?" I hated saying her name with such uncertainty when I felt it in my gut that was who she was, but my voice wasn't my own. It was too weak sounding, too shaken up.

"Yeah, that's Jane Hawker," Eli said.

Sickness sloshed through my stomach. I felt like Benji, just waiting to hurl any second.

"Why was she here in the park?" I asked once I was able to find my voice again. "Was she here to see us?"

It didn't make sense because Jane was a human. She wouldn't know we were werewolves. Even if she suspected it, why waste your final moments trying to get to us?

"I have no clue," Eli insisted.

The sirens grew closer. They were almost upon us. I could see their lights in the distance. The blue and red bounced off Mr. Russell's trailer.

Was Officer Dan going to make it here before anyone else to look over the scene and come up with a story that didn't reek of something suspicious?

An ominous feeling settled over me. "Do you think she was planning to warn us about something?" The Midnight Reaper perhaps.

"I don't know what she would be warning us about; she was human. One who couldn't have known for sure what we were." Eli's voice was soft, respectful. Still, his words stung.

I hated that he had discredited Jane coming to warn us about something simply because she was human. I knew I'd made the same judgment seconds before, but now it didn't seem right.

Her being human didn't mean anything. She still could've had a message for us. She could have known what we were and thought of us as her salvation.

If that was the case, we'd failed her.

Even if it wasn't, I'd failed her.

I should've pushed harder for the pack to visit her. I should've gone on my own. I should've asked her the questions I wanted. I should've listened to her rendition of what happened that night. Instead, I'd listened to Eli. Next time I'd listen to myself. I'd do what I thought was necessary.

However, I hoped like hell there would never be a next time. I hoped the Midnight Reaper would be caught and brought to justice.

An ambulance made its way toward us. Paramedics hopped out the instant it stopped. There was nothing they could do for Jane. She was already gone. Still they tried.

The police showed up next. Officer Dan was among them. He stepped to Dorian and Eli. Questions were tossed between the men, but I didn't pay them any mind. My focus was on the body of Jane Hawker.

She hadn't deserved to die. She'd only been in the wrong place at the wrong time.

Officer Dan bent to touch his fingertips to her eyelids, closing them when the paramedics had given up on trying to revive her. Somehow, this made her seem at peace. I truly hoped she was after everything she'd had to endure. My gaze drifted to Eli. His arms were folded across his chest in a stiff way as he stared down at her. His brows pinched together in sadness, but the longer I stared at him, the more I noticed another emotion surfacing in his features.

Curiosity.

What was he staring at with such interest?

"Wait!" Eli moved closer to Jane's body. He bent at

the waist and pushed up the sleeve of her nightgown. "There's something here."

Words decorated the inside of her arm. My stomach flip-flopped as I took in the rusty liquid they'd been written in. Was that blood? Her blood? Had she wrote on herself, or had someone wrote a message on her?

I stepped forward, needing a closer look.

"What the hell?" Dorian peered over Eli's shoulder. "What's it say?"

"Your alpha is mine," I answered when Eli didn't. My voice shook from the fast pounding of my heart as I continued to stare at the words.

This couldn't be something Jane had wrote on herself. She didn't know about us. She didn't know about our alpha. It had to be a message from the Midnight Reaper. But what did it mean? Was our alpha really in danger?

"It's a trap," Eli insisted. He stood and scanned the woods. "She was a diversion. This was all a trap for my dad."

How? Why? My mind raced with multiple questions.

"Where's your dad?" Officer Dan asked.

"He went to search the woods with some others," Eli said. "He thought the one responsible might still be close by."

"We should make sure they're okay," Dorian insisted.

Eli swung around to face me. His eyes were dark and cold. Whatever horrible thoughts I was thinking were obviously no match for his.

"I'll be back as soon as we find them," he said.

I didn't want him to go, but I knew he had to. He

needed to make sure his dad and the others were okay. I understood that, even if I didn't like it.

I licked my lips. "Be careful." I pulled him in for a hug and a quick kiss on the cheek.

"Make sure you call or text me if you find them," Officer Dan insisted, breaking up the fragile moment I was stuck in with Eli. "I'll stay back and figure out a way to cover this up. I doubt anyone else noticed it, or else they would have said something. The coroner will find it though if I don't get rid of it, and then it will be hard to make the claim of an animal attack or another victim of the Midnight Reaper stick."

"I'll get you a rag or something to clean it off." I rushed back to the building without glancing at Eli again. I didn't want him to see how worried I was to have him leave my sight. To have him going out there with that monster on the loose.

"Is everything okay out there?" Gran asked when I entered the building.

"No. That was Jane Hawker," I said in a low voice as I spotted Ridley, Benji, Alec, and Becca in the back of the building. Somehow Ridley must have been able to get them inside. "She's dead."

"Oh my goodness. I knew something was going to happen today. I could feel it." Gran placed a hand on my back.

"I did too," I admitted.

"Do we know what happened to her yet?" Mom asked. Her voice was low, but I knew the pack could hear her even if my human friends couldn't.

"We think it was the work of the Midnight Reaper," I said. "I need a rag. Or a napkin. Something."

Gasps echoed around me as murmurings of what I'd said rang through the pack. I hoped no one mentioned vampires and it got to the ears of my friends. I especially hoped no one repeated what I was about to say next.

"What do you need a napkin for?" Gran asked as she handed me a stack.

"There was a message written on the inside of her arm," I said as I took them from her. "It said 'your alpha is mine'."

"Oh dear," Gran whispered.

Alec said something to me, but I ignored him. He shouldn't be here. Neither should Becca or Benji. They needed to go. The party was over.

I glanced at Ridley, hoping to convey this without words. She nodded in understanding, and I headed back outside with a stack of napkins to help Officer Dan.

11

Once Officer Dan discreetly wiped the message on Jane's arm off, he motioned for the coroner to take her away. The guy hadn't been paying attention. Thank goodness.

The coroner pronounced Jane dead and named her time of death. Then, she was carried away.

"Make sure someone calls me when the others return," Officer Dan insisted, his hand on my shoulder. "I'd like to know Wesley and the others are okay."

I nodded. "Yeah, sure. I will." I folded my arms over my chest, unable to shake the cold chill that had gripped hold of me since seeing Jane carried away. "Thanks for helping to clean that up before anyone else saw."

"No problem," Officer Dan said as he walked away.

I stared at the space where Jane's body had been moments before. A pool of blood stained the gravel, and there were droplets of it leading up to it from the woods.

Police were walking through the woods, searching for whatever creature Officer Dan had told them to be on the lookout for. It was clear they weren't really trying to find anything though. They probably thought the sirens had scared away the animal.

"Someone should clean that up so the little kids don't see," Alec said. I jumped, not having heard him come up behind me. My mind was elsewhere. "Not that they haven't already seen worse tonight, but still."

"Yeah," I whispered. The park was clearing out, which meant everyone would be leaving the party building and heading back to their trailers. Alec should leave too. He shouldn't have been here to begin with.

"I don't know how you clean up something like that." He crammed his hands in the front pockets of his jeans.

"Me either."

My gaze drifted back to the puddle of blood.

I didn't know Jane, but I felt as though I did. There was a hole inside me because of her death. One where guilt had made itself a home. While I knew I shouldn't feel responsible for what happened to her, I did.

"Oh, honey," Mom said as she came up behind me. She pulled me in for a hug and I let her. "I'm so sorry your birthday ended this way."

"Me too," I said, even though I'd forgotten it was my birthday. The party and fun seemed like it happened forever ago.

"They'll catch whoever did this. The alp–" Dad coughed. I knew it was because he'd been about to say something about our alpha, and then realized he was in

Alec's presence. "The police will nab whoever's responsible."

I hoped he was right. I hoped the alpha ripped his damn throat out. All of them. My wolf wished for the same.

No. Our alpha needed to stay as far away from the Midnight Reaper.

Vampire. Alpha. Death threat.

These three thoughts circled through my mind while Mom continued to talk. I couldn't focus on what she was saying. My mind was somewhere else.

I was back in the city with Regina. She'd just told me the reason she was seeking revenge against my pack, against my alpha.

Your alpha is mine.

The words flashed through my mind again, written in Jane's blood on her arm.

"No," I whispered. "It can't be her."

"Can't be who, honey?" Mom asked. "What are you talking about?"

I licked my lips. "No one. It's nothing. Forget it. I'm just tired."

"Understandable," Mom insisted. "You could come home with us until Eli comes back."

Eli.

What if it was Regina responsible for all of this somehow? What would she do to Eli?

My heart pounded in my chest as possible scenarios played through my mind. None of them were good.

It couldn't be her though, I tried to rationalize. I'd watched her die. I'd crammed multiple syringes of

Abstraction into her system, flooding it. Then, I'd watched as she overdosed. Next, Eli had staked her. She'd turned to ashes. I saw her.

No. It couldn't be her. It couldn't even be about her. It had to be someone else.

But who?

"Honey?" Mom pressed.

"I'll be okay. I'm going to go home and wait for Eli," I said as I smoothed a hand over my forehead.

"Care for any company?" Alec asked.

My eyes snapped to him as my teeth sank into my bottom lip. I knew I should say no, but for whatever reason, I couldn't bring myself to.

"Sure," I said.

The ghost of a smile crossed Alec's face. "Cool."

"Umm, well. We'll be at home if you need us," Mom insisted. She pulled me in for another hug before she and Dad started home.

"Happy birthday," Dad called over his shoulder.

I waved and flashed a small smile before I started walking to my trailer with Alec at my side. We didn't get far before Gracie called out to me.

"Hey. Do you want me to take Moonshine home with me?" she asked, hugging my puppy to her chest. How could I have forgotten about her?

"No. It's okay. I'll take her." I reached for her as soon as Gracie was close enough. "Thanks, though."

"No problem. I'll, uh, talk to you later." She wanted to talk about what happened. I could see her questions burning in her eyes.

In that moment, I was glad Alec stood beside me. He

was serving as a shield, allowing me to not have to talk about the things that had happened with Jane.

"Yeah. Okay," I said as I squeezed Moonshine against my chest. She wiggled, wanting down, but I refused to set her down.

I glanced behind me to see if anyone else waited to say something and spotted Ridley and Benji coming out of the party building with Becca. Benji looked as though he still wasn't feeling well. Concern for him shifted across Ridley's face while Becca looked as though she were in shock.

"Hey, I'm sorry to dip out, but I think Benji needs to go home and lie down," Ridley said as they made their way to where Alec and I stood.

"I just can't get over all that blood," Benji whispered. His eyes drifted between Alec and me to the pool of blood on the gravel. "Oh, man, there it is again. I think I'm gonna be sick!" His hand flew to his mouth as his cheeks puffed out. He dashed to the nearest trash can.

"It's okay. I'll call you later," I said as I motioned for Ridley to follow him.

"Happy birthday," she shouted over her shoulder as she ran to where Benji hunched over a trash can.

"I think I'm going to head home too," Becca said. She folded her arms across her chest as a shiver slipped through her body, her expression haunted. "This has got me all freaked out." Her gaze darted to the woods as though she were waiting for something to jump out and attack her.

"I know. Me too. Thanks for coming though." I

reached out to give her a one-armed hug. Moonshine wiggled to get away from us both.

"Happy birthday," Becca insisted as she returned my hug. "I'll try to swing by and see you before I leave tomorrow."

"Maybe we can meet for breakfast or something?"

"I'd like that." She touched Alec's arm. "I'll talk to you later too."

"Can you make it home okay? I can drive you if you need me to," Alec offered, always a gentleman.

"I'll be all right," she said as she started toward where she'd parked.

A few members of the pack whispered happy birthday to me as they started to their trailers, ready to turn in for the night. I set Moonshine on the ground and walked Alec toward Eli's and my trailer, still wondering if asking him to stay was stupid.

"You okay?" he asked once we are almost to the front door.

"As okay as I can be, considering," I said without looking at him. "What about you?"

"Same." He scratched the back of his neck. "That was crazy."

"Yeah, it was," I said even though he didn't know the half of it.

We started up the wooden stairs to my place, and I opened the door. Eli's familiar scent lingered in the air. Worry shifted through me. What if he didn't come back? What if something horrible happened while he was in the woods? What if the Midnight Reaper got him?

My heartbeat grew sluggish as my mind continued to crank out one horrible thought after the other. I should've gone with him. Simple as that.

What the hell was I doing here with Alec?

There wasn't anything romantic left between us. Ivette had seen to making me a friend and nothing more in his eyes when she screwed with his memory, and I was imprinted with Eli. There was no room for anyone else inside my heart. There never would be.

So, why had I told him he could stay?

Alec reminded me of a different part of myself, one that was separate from anything supernatural. To me, he represented normalcy. That was why I'd invited him to stay. My mind needed normalcy on this crazy night.

If not, I'd worry myself sick. Especially now with Eli in the woods with that monster.

"Wow, this place is nice," Alec said as he followed me inside and closed the door behind him.

"Thanks," I muttered as I unhooked Moonshine from her leash.

She ran straight to Alec and sniffed his boots.

"She's cute." He bent down to pet her. "What did you say her name was again?"

"Moonshine."

"Interesting name."

"Eli came up with it. It's mainly because of the white circle on top of her head. It sort of looks like a moon."

"Yeah, I guess. I probably would've named her Luna or something though."

A smile twisted at the corners of my lips because that was exactly what I'd said to Eli when we first got her.

"Are you thirsty?" I asked as I stepped to the kitchen to get myself a glass of water.

"No, I'm fine."

I grabbed a glass from the cabinet beside the sink and filled it with tap water. Alec was still petting Moonshine when I turned back around. She licked his hand.

"I think you made a new friend," I said, watching the two of them.

"I think so." Alec chuckled. "So, when do you think Eli will be back?"

"I don't know." Worry bubbled through me again. "Hopefully soon."

Alec stood, abandoning petting Moonshine. She jumped on him and yipped, not having it. "Do you think he'll be okay with my being here?"

"Yeah. You're my friend. He knows that."

Relief registered in Alec's eyes. "Cool. I didn't want to cause any friction between the two of you, especially after everything that's happened tonight already."

"It'll be okay." I slipped past him and stepped into the living room, heading for the couch. Alec followed and moved to sit beside me. He scratched at his eyebrow as he situated himself. I studied his face, trying to determine what he was thinking.

"What do you think happened to that girl?" he asked.

I should have known that was where his mind was. Alec always was the curious type.

"I'm not sure."

"Her neck looked as though it had been mauled," he whispered. "Like something had viciously attacked her."

I was treading in dangerous territory, which meant I needed to be careful with what I said next.

"I know," I said, hoping agreeing with him and not adding anything else would suffice enough to end the conversation.

"So, what do you think attacked her?" he pressed. Did he think I knew something more than him? Could he sense it? I tried to get a vibe off where he was going with all of this but couldn't. Alec was hard to read. "It had to be an animal of some kind."

Moonshine jumped up onto the couch and settled between us. I reached out to stroke the crown of her head, giving myself a moment to think of an answer.

"Maybe it was a bear." I shrugged.

"Maybe," Alec said. "I guess it could've swiped at her if she'd startled it somehow."

"Yeah."

"I didn't get a chance to look at the rest of her to see if there were other marks. Did you?"

"I think there was something on her leg. Possibly on her midsection too," I lied. If he thought there was more than one wound, maybe the animal theory would hold better clout with him.

Hopefully when Officer Dan filed the report, he noted that an animal attack was the cause of death. That was what needed to be circulated through town because I knew it would somehow find its way back to Alec. I didn't want him harboring any questions about tonight.

"God, that's got to be an awful way to go," Alec said. A breath of air rushed past his lips, and he smoothed a hand along his face. His eyes locked with mine when it fell to his lap again. "What if it was that serial killer? The Midnight Reaper? I remember seeing on the news another body was found about thirty miles from here this morning."

Shit. He was putting pieces together, but it wasn't his puzzle to complete.

"I heard about that too. It's possible the Midnight Reaper might be in town, I guess. Although, I seriously hope not," I said before chugging some of my water. I needed to stop talking. I wasn't helping the situation.

"Markings on her arms and legs would make sense if it were the Midnight Reaper too. They said in one of the reports some of the bodies had been mutilated."

He was looking too deep into this. I needed to change the subject.

"If she ran through the woods, she could've had plenty of scratches on her arms and legs, whether she was running from an animal or the killer," I said as I reached for the TV remote. "Do you want to watch some TV? We have Netflix."

Alec didn't speak. I knew him well enough to know it was because he was mulling over the possibilities of both theories being true.

I set my water on the coffee table and scrolled through comedies. I decided on one I hadn't seen in forever and pulled Moonshine into my lap.

Time ticked away.

When the movie was almost over, a pang of worry slithered through me. I still hadn't heard from Eli. Just when I thought to get up and grab my cell so I could send him a text asking if he was okay, the front door swung open and he stumbled in.

Blood and grime marred his beautiful skin, and his clothes were in tatters.

12

Eli nearly collapsed as he stepped through the door. Moonshine darted to him, eager to greet him, but he ignored her. Instead, he closed the door behind him with more force than necessary, causing both Alec and me to jump. I was on my feet, eyes wide, and rushing toward him seconds later.

"Eli!" I shouted. "What happened?"

"Are you okay, man?" Alec asked.

"No." Eli shifted his gaze to him.

His eyes were cold and hard, but I could tell his anger was about to crumble any moment. Something else was poking through the surface of his features. Knots formed in my stomach. Whatever was wrong, it was bad. I could tell. Too many emotions rippled off him for it not to be. Even my wolf was on edge from them.

"What happened?" I tried again.

I reached out for him. My fingers brushed his face,

his neck, his arms in their search for any injuries but finding none.

The blood wasn't his.

Whose was it then?

"My dad," Eli started and then stopped.

His eyes lifted to mine. The skin around them bunched as though he were in pain. A lump formed in my throat. I knew what he was about to say.

"He's gone. My dad is gone," Eli muttered. His pupils became dilated as his face took on an ashy look. I imagined images of whatever he'd witnessed in the woods were flooding his mind. "*Gone.*"

I reached out and pulled him into a hug. All I wanted was to ease his pain, even though I knew it wouldn't be possible. Physical touch couldn't cure the heart or mind when it came to something like this no matter how much we wished it were true.

"I should probably get going," Alec said from somewhere behind me. I'd forgotten he was here. "I'm sorry for your loss, man. I really am. I'll call or text you later, Mina."

"Okay," I said, unwilling to let Eli go.

Alec stepped to where I stood, embracing Eli, and gave him a soft pat on the back before disappearing through the front door. I was glad he'd taken it upon himself to leave because I imagined whatever Eli had to say next wasn't something Alec should hear.

"Tell me what happened," I insisted, pressing for details. "Is everyone else okay?"

Eli's grip on me tightened. I hated myself for asking,

but I needed to know details. I had to know everyone else was okay.

"It was all a diversion like I thought. A trap," he said as he unwound himself from me and wiped his nose with the back of his hand. "By the time we caught up with my dad and the rest of the pack, it was too late."

My stomach somersaulted. What? No! Everyone couldn't be dead.

I tried to think of who had gone into the woods with Eli's dad.

Frank, Sabin, and Glenn.

Eli's brows pinched together. "A couple of the guys were hurt, but my dad..."

"Was gone when you got there," I finished for him in a whisper.

Tears built in Eli's bright green eyes, magnifying their color as he nodded. I glanced away, unable to bear to looking at him, seeing his pain. I felt it stronger than I thought possible through the imprint. My vision blurred as tears formed in my eyes.

"His throat was ripped out, Mina. There was blood everywhere." His voice shook when he spoke. My hands reached out to cup his face. Eli leaned into my touch, and my wolf let out a howl. She was as heartbroken as I was to see him this way. To learn the news of our alpha. "There was something written on his arm. Just like Jane's."

My skin tingled as the heavy feeling in my stomach spread.

"What did it say?"

"One down," Eli said through gritted teeth.

One down? What did that mean? Was this vampire planning to kill our pack members one by one? Was he planning to kill all supernaturals in town? If that were the case, then the Montevallos and the Caraways were at risk as well.

A sob shook Eli's body, pulling my attention back to him.

"I'm so sorry," I breathed.

"He wasn't supposed to die that way. Not like that," Eli said. "He just wasn't."

More tears filled his eyes. I'd never seen Eli cry before. He was always so sure and calm. Not emotionless or heartless but strong. Tough.

In this situation, however, Eli was broken and he had every right to be.

Tears burned my eyes as I held him close. His body shuddered as he let go and gave in to what he was feeling fully.

"I'm so sorry," I whispered again, because it was the only thing I knew to say.

"I had to tell my mom. She saw me coming out of the woods and ran to ask if everything was okay." I could feel his chin tremble as he spoke. "It didn't feel real telling her. It didn't feel like I was speaking. This feels like a nightmare I can't wake from, Mina. Why can't I wake up? This can't be real."

My heart broke for him. I wanted to make his pain stop but knew it wasn't possible. Or was it?

Would the youngest Montevallo sister, Ivette, be able to compel Eli to forget the pain of his father's death? Would he be interested in that?

"I can't believe this," Eli said as he untangled himself

from my arms. "I just...I can't." He wiped at his eyes and smeared the blood and grime caking his skin.

I stepped into the kitchen and grabbed a wad of paper towels. I wet them at the sink.

"One down," Eli whispered. "What does that even mean? I need to figure it out. I have to stop this freaking vampire before he hurts anyone else. Most of all, I need revenge."

I licked my lips and stared at him. His eyes were wild. His jaw tense. His hands were fisted at his sides. With the blood and grime caked across his face, Eli looked like a madman.

"Help me figure this out, Mina. Please. I need to know what you think the message on my father meant."

A haunted look entered his eyes. It had me on edge. I ignored the pricking of my scalp and stepped forward to clean him up.

"I don't know," I said as I smoothed the wet paper towel across his face. "It could mean he's planning to take out pack members one by one, or he's targeting the supernaturals of Mirror Lake."

"You're right. We should warn the others, just in case it's the latter."

"The others?" I asked when he didn't specify.

"Everyone. The pack. The Montevallos. The Caraways. Everyone should be on their toes." He paced back and forth, his off-kilter energy vibrating around him.

Eli needed a release.

Something to divert his pent-up energy. I doubted I'd be able to encourage him to go for a run, even though that would be the most helpful. If his man was this distraught, his wolf was worse.

Crafting a plan of action might work, though.

"You should set up a meeting sometime tomorrow with Dorian and the others," I suggested. "Also, someone should be in contact with the Montevallos and the Caraways to fill them in on things."

"That's a good idea." Eli nodded, but still continued to pace. His hands moved to his head where his fingers tugged at his hair. "Damn it! I can't be here anymore. I need to be doing something."

"Like what?" I asked, shocked he'd resorted to yelling. Eli hardly raised his voice. Especially when he was angry.

"I need to be out there." He pointed at the front door. "I need to be searching the woods, trying to find a clue as to who this is we're dealing with." He grabbed the flashlight from the junk drawer in the kitchen and his cell before I could figure out something to say that would make him stay.

"I'm coming with you," I said when I couldn't think of a good enough reason.

Eli paused at the door and glanced back at me.

"No. You're not coming. There's something horrible out there, Mina," he said.

I folded my arms over my chest. Was he really pulling this crap with me?

"Like that's ever stopped me before," I muttered, trying to play hardball with him. I wasn't sure it would work this time. He was unhinged.

The corners of his lips worked into the ghost of a smile, surprising me. "Fine, stubborn ass, but we have to be careful," Eli insisted. "I mean it. For all we know, the Midnight Reaper could be out there still, waiting to ambush us like he did my father."

"I know. I'll be careful, but I'm not letting you go out there alone."

I grabbed my cell off the kitchen counter and followed Eli. The trailer park was quiet as we started down the wooden steps and cut toward the woods. I imagined the rest of the pack was trying to process the events of the night. Had word traveled that our alpha had passed? My wolf howled at the reminder. I could feel her sorrow pulsing through me, adding to my own.

"Use the flashlight on your cell," Eli insisted, glancing over his shoulder to look at me. "Be on the lookout for blood, scratches on the ground, anything. That filthy vampire had to leave something behind. Jane wasn't just deposited in the park from thin air; she had to have walked from somewhere."

"Didn't your dad and the others follow a trail from her earlier?" I asked, remembering the blood splatters across the gravel behind Jane's body that led into the woods.

"The trail stopped inside the woods. There wasn't much to follow."

I stepped into the thick foliage behind him. A cool wind kicked up, unraveling hair from the bun on top of my head and chilling me. I should've grabbed a light jacket.

"There." Eli positioned his flashlight on a patch of ground a few feet in front of us. "That's where Jane's blood trail ends."

I stared at the drops of red blood splattered across bits of gravel and clumps of dirt. My stomach quivered.

"Watch where you step," Eli insisted. "We don't want to destroy evidence while we're out here."

"This isn't my first rodeo."

Eli glanced at me from over his shoulder. Even in the moonlight, I could see his eyes soften.

"I know. I'm sorry," he said.

I licked my lips as I held his stare. "It's okay."

"It's not. I'm being an ass."

"Well, at least you can admit it." I grinned.

"I can," he insisted. "Thanks for coming out here with me."

"You know I'm here for you."

He nodded. "I know."

We walked side by side as we made our way through the woods. Memories of the last time we'd tramped through the woods together at night flashed through my mind. We'd been searching for clues in regards to Glenn's disappearance.

God, that seemed like so long ago.

Another gust of wind blew as we walked deeper into the woods. A scrap of white fabric stuck to a bare tree branch caught my attention as it flapped in the wind.

Was it a piece of Jane's nightgown?

I started toward it against my wolf's advice. She wanted me to stay by Eli's side, but I ignored her.

When I reached the tree, movement at my left caught my eye.

Adrenaline flooded my system. I froze and glanced around, searching for whatever it might have been, but there was nothing there. I held my breath and listened. All I could hear was Eli. He was hunched down, brushing his fingertips against the ground, seeming as though he may have found something else.

A twig snapped behind me.

I spun around barely fast enough to catch the tail end of a person. They were too fast for me to tell if they were male or female. My wolf nudged me, reminding me that their gender didn't matter. What mattered was someone was in the woods with us.

The question was: Who? Was it the Midnight Reaper?

I eyed the section of the woods I'd seen them disappear in. Either they were hiding, or they'd moved on. With shaky legs, I moved to the scrap of fabric dangling in the tree. I pulled it from the branch and noticed there was a smear of blood staining it.

"What's that?" Eli asked. His sudden close proximity had me jumping. He reached out for me. "Sorry, I didn't mean to scare you. It looks like you found something, though."

"Yeah." I held out the scrap of fabric. "I think it's a piece of Jane's nightgown. There's a smear of blood on the edge. It might be hers. Also, I think there's someone out here with us."

"Where?" Eli glanced around. "I don't see anyone."

"They're gone now, at least I think they are, but they were fast. Like vampire fast," I said.

"We should get out of here, then," Eli insisted.

The instant he said something, I could pick up on the

sensation of someone watching me. Whatever it was, the eyes didn't feel friendly.

Cold chills swept up my spine as my wolf fought to take over.

"Stay close." Eli gripped my forearm and pulled me behind him. "It was a bad idea to come out here tonight. I should have never agreed to bring you with me."

I didn't argue because I wasn't one hundred percent focused on what he was saying. Instead, my attention was fixed on scanning the woods for whatever was watching us. Chills crept along my spine as I realized yet again that something sinister lurked in the Mirror Lake woods.

13

I woke to the sound of a fist pounding on something. I wasn't sure what time it was or how I'd ended up in bed. The last thing I remembered was being on the couch with Eli after we came back from the woods. We'd been talking about what we found, who might have been watching us, and coming up with ideas for how Jane might've gotten to the park. When I thought I'd seen someone, Eli had been examining the ground where he found a large splatter of blood. We'd been pinging ideas off each other when my eyes grew heavy, but our theory was Jane had been attacked while she was in the woods. I must've dozed off shortly after we came to the conclusion.

How did I get here, then? Had Eli carried me to bed?

The pounding came again, startling me.

Was someone beating on our front door? Or was the noise coming from somewhere inside the trailer?

I flung my blankets off and slipped out of bed. Every

light in the trailer seemed to be on as I entered the hallway.

"Damn it," I heard Eli mutter. "This just doesn't make any sense."

"What doesn't?" I asked as I entered the living room.

What was he still doing up?

My gaze skimmed the room. Crumpled papers littered the floor. Throw pillows had been tossed around. And a hand-drawn map took up most of the coffee table in front of Eli. There was a spiderweb of red lines and circles marking up its surface that drew my attention. I tried to make sense of what I was looking at but was unable to figure it out. My gaze drifted to the laptop beside Eli, its screen still glowing as though he'd set it aside for a second.

"Have you been up all night?" I asked as I continued toward where he was sitting.

Eli didn't look at me. He scooped the laptop up and placed it in his lap. His index finger and thumb worked the mouse pad in the center as his brows furrowed.

"I couldn't sleep. I need to figure this out," he said.

"Figure what out? What are you doing? And what's the map of?" I asked as I moved to sit beside him.

"The killings. There's no rhyme or reason. Some of the victims were drained while others were mutilated," Eli insisted as he clicked around on the computer. "Some of them were toyed with as though it was all a game, like Jane. I don't understand. If this were a true serial killer, there would be a link between the murders, but there isn't."

I tucked my legs beneath me as my gaze skimmed

over the giant map he'd drawn, taking in every circle and line he'd created.

"That just proves what we thought earlier, doesn't it? There's more than one person? More than one vampire?" I suggested.

Eli shifted to look at me. "You're right. For whatever reason I've been set in thinking it was one vampire again." His attention shifted back to his computer. "This could be the work of multiple vampires. An entire group. They could be doing this all for the hell of it." Eli's body vibrated with rage.

While I was glad to help, I hoped I was wrong. A group of vampires hell-bent on killing and massacring people for the fun of it wasn't something I wanted to encounter.

Ever.

"It's almost six," Eli insisted as he closed out tabs on his laptop and shut it down. "I need to call Dorian and the others to set up a meeting this morning. Explain my theories and create a better plan. I want this vampire, or group of vampires, stopped today."

I stared at the dark circles under his eyes. "Are you sure you don't want to get some sleep, and maybe something to eat first?"

Eli shook his head and closed the laptop. "I don't need sleep or food. I need to find the person responsible for murdering my father."

I swallowed hard. "Okay. Let me get dressed before you invite everyone over," I said as I headed to our room. Eli didn't respond. Instead, he got up to gather the papers he'd tossed around.

My teeth sank into my bottom lip as I walked down the hall. I didn't know how to be supportive in a situation like this. It was new territory. I pulled on a pair of jeans and a T-shirt, then reached for a hair tie from on top of our dresser. When I started back down the hall, Eli was already on the phone with someone.

I had no idea who he was talking to, but I could guess. Dorian was his second. They'd grown close since everything with Regina in the city.

A whimper came from the opposite side of the living room. Moonshine. A towel had been placed over her crate in the corner so Eli's light wouldn't bother her. I crossed the living room, ready to take her outside.

When I came back in, Eli was off the phone and sitting on the couch with his feet propped up on the coffee table. His head was in his hands.

I closed the door behind me and bent to release Moonshine from her leash. "Everything okay?"

"Yeah," Eli said as he shifted to stare at me. "Dorian and some of the others will be over in a few minutes."

"Okay. I'm sure you'll feel better once you talk things out with the others," I said.

"We'll see."

"How are the others? Frank, Sabin, and Glenn were with your dad. You said they were hurt. Are they okay now?" I prayed they were. I couldn't bear to think of losing another pack member.

"They're fine," Eli insisted as he leaned back against the couch. "Werewolf healing."

I crossed to the kitchen and placed Moonshine's leash on the counter, before contemplating what I wanted for breakfast and pouring myself a glass of orange juice. The desire to ask if Eli wanted me to make him something built on the tip of my tongue. I didn't ask though because he had already said he wasn't hungry. I didn't want to push the issue.

Opting for a bowl of cereal, I leaned against the kitchen counter and tried not to stare at him as he looked at the map sprawled across our coffee table. He was adding things to a smaller map while mumbling to himself when a knock sounded at the front door.

"Come in," Eli shouted. He didn't look up from the maps.

The door opened and Dorian stepped inside. Moonshine jumped off the couch and bolted straight to him. I chuckled at the way her tongue flipped out of her mouth while she ran.

"Aw, hello there, cutie," Dorian said as he bent down to scratch behind her ear. His gaze drifted to Eli when he straightened himself. Sympathy worked its way into his features before he shifted his gaze to me. He swallowed hard and nodded. I was positive he could feel the tension rippling off Eli and was asking without words if he was okay. I nodded in reply before he started toward Eli. "The others will be here any second. I saw Frank headed this way before I knocked."

"Good," Eli insisted without looking up from his maps. "We have a lot to discuss."

Dorian nodded, but he didn't speak. Instead, he folded his arms over his chest and studied Eli. I got the impression he wanted to say something, but he wasn't sure how to word it properly.

Another knock sounded at the door. I was glad because whatever Dorian was about to say I didn't think Eli would enjoy hearing it.

"It's open," Eli shouted.

Frank stepped inside, followed by Sabin, Max, Glenn, and Dorian's dad, Charles. I finished the rest of my cereal as I watched the men congregate in my living room. They waited for Eli to say something, to let them know why they were here, but he refused to be bothered. Instead, he continued marking on his map.

I rinsed my bowl in the kitchen sink as another knock sounded at the front door. Wasn't everyone here? Who else could Eli have called?

Eli glanced up from what he was doing and took in those around him for the first time. The same thought must have crossed his mind because his brows pinched together.

Whoever was at the door knocked a second time, this time louder than the first.

"Come in," Eli insisted.

Tate stepped inside. I wasn't sure who I'd been expecting to see, but the sight of him had my tense muscles relaxing.

"I thought everyone was coming this way. Figures you'd hold a damn meeting without me," Tate said through gritted teeth, his gaze locked on Eli. "I want to be here. I want to be a part of this. Whatever it is. Don't you dare deny me."

Tension rippled through the room as Tate and Eli began a silent stare down. No one spoke. We were all waiting to hear Eli's reply. I hoped he didn't send Tate away. He had every right to be here. Yes, he was young, but he was hurting as bad as Eli. He was also as much a part of this pack as the rest of us.

"Fine," Eli insisted as he continued to stare at Tate with cold, dark eyes. It was clear he didn't like being told what to do in front of everyone, especially not when it came from his kid brother, but it was also clear he understood Tate's demand.

Next to Eli, Tate was the oldest of the Vargas boys. He also was the one who was most similar to Eli. They both held a ferocious desire to protect those they cared about and to seek justice for those taken from them too soon.

The Midnight Reaper had no clue whom he'd screwed with.

Tate swallowed hard. He licked his lips, and I swore I saw relief trickle through his features.

"Okay, now that everyone's here," Eli said. His eyes narrowed as he glanced around the room. "We have some important things to discuss. You all are well aware of what happened to my father—our alpha—yesterday, and that it was a vampire responsible."

Everyone in the room nodded, but no one spoke.

As sad as it was, we all knew what the death of our alpha meant—Eli was alpha now. It didn't matter that he hadn't made it through the rite ceremony yet, which was customary; he was still the alpha. It was his birthright. Everyone could feel that the shift of power had already been made. It rippled off Eli in waves, intensified by the rage and heartbreak echoing through him.

"Mina and I went into the woods last night to search for clues—"

"That was a dumb idea," Dorian interrupted. "What were you thinking? You saw what this thing can do. It wiped out your dad like he was nothing. He didn't even have a chance against him."

My gaze drifted to Dorian. How could he say something so insensitive? The desire to reach out and smack him pulsed through me.

Charles, Dorian's dad, nudged him. "Respect, Dorian. Have a little respect."

Dorian dropped his chin. "I'm sorry."

"I couldn't stay here. I couldn't just sit here. I had to do something," Eli insisted.

"Did you find anything?" Tate asked.

Eli shook his head. "Not really, no. We found a scrap of Jane's nightgown with a smear of blood on it, and we also learned she was attacked in the woods, or at least that's our thought. There was a puddle of blood."

"So what, this thing lured her into the woods?" Sabin asked.

"I think so," Eli insisted.

Max huffed. "What a sick fu—"

"I know," Eli said. "In my research last night, there seemed to be a couple of instances where the victim was toyed with before being killed. At least ten of them. The rest were split between being mutilated or drained."

"What did he do, play eeny meeny miny moe to decide which victims were going to receive which torture?" Max asked. Disgust dripped from his words.

"Is there a strategy? Like a way to tell what he'll do

next based off his previous victims?" Dorian asked before Eli could respond to Max.

"I thought all night about how this might be the doings of one vampire and why he'd bounce from one horrific way to kill someone to another. It didn't make sense," Eli insisted. He pointed to the big map in front of him. "This is the U.S. I checked worldwide, but there didn't seem to be any killings in other countries by the Midnight Reaper, at least none reported on mainstream media. It looks as though he started in Los Angeles and made his way across the United States. The problem is there doesn't seem to be any rhyme or reason as to how he's killing people, which leads me to believe there might be more than one killer involved. More than one vampire."

"A pack of mindless bloodsucking vampires," Tate spat. "Great, I'm sure that's exactly what everyone wanted to hear."

"It makes sense to think there's more than one," Max said.

"It does, but it doesn't tell us how many we could potentially be dealing with," Frank insisted. His gaze dipped to the map. "How many were you thinking?"

"Based on everything I've looked at, it seems we might be dealing with three or four vampires."

"Did any of you happen to see how many were out there yesterday when you searched the woods after the incident with Jane?" Dorian glanced around the room.

"Already told you, they were fast as hell. Definitely not afraid to use vampy speed," Glenn insisted.

Was he insinuating they were faster than a regular

vampire? Was that what I saw last night? A super fast vampire? Or was it something else entirely?

"The speed made it hard to distinguish if there was more than one vampire present," Sabin said.

"So, there could have been more than one out there with you?" I asked, thinking we were right.

"I can't guarantee it, but it would make damn good sense." Sabin nodded.

"Okay, so. What do we know about vampires?" Dorian asked as he folded his arms over his chest and paced the living room. Moonshine followed behind him like his shadow. "We know they can have special powers, which means there's a possibility this one has increased speed."

"Is that even a thing?" I asked. "I mean, I guess it could be. I just figured vampires are fast anyway. Why would one be super fast?"

"Why not?" Eli countered. "Look at the Montevallos. We know they each have special powers. Why shouldn't others? Even Regina held the power of compulsion."

"I'm not saying the Midnight Reaper couldn't potentially have some sort of power," I said. "What I'm saying is I don't think super speed counts since they already have that ability regularly."

Eli's eyes locked on me. "I don't think it's something we should discredit yet."

"All right," I said, granting him that. "So, if this vampire has super speed, could he have potentially killed all of those people by himself?"

"Why are you suddenly back to there being one killer?" Glenn asked.

My mind shifted to a paranormal book Gracie had told me she'd read once. It was about a vampire who was haunted by his past. He went around killing people and tormenting them as though he were locked in the mind of this vicious form of his prior self, unable to break free.

My gut was telling me this might be something similar.

"I'm just trying out all of the possibilities," I insisted. "There's a chance this could be one vampire we're dealing with. One who's haunted by his past. Maybe there were three ways he chose to kill his victims over the last hundred, or hundreds, of years."

Silence built through the trailer.

"Why now, though?" Tate asked. It is clear he was taking my new theory into consideration.

I shrugged. "Why not? Maybe something changed. Maybe someone he loved passed away. Who knows? All I'm saying is that there's a good chance this could still be one vampire since no one can say for sure."

I liked the idea of it being one. We would have a better chance of killing it then.

"I say we visit the Montevallos and see if they know anything about all of this," Dorian insisted.

"I think you're right," Eli agreed with a nod his head. "We need to rework the patrol schedule now that the Midnight Reaper has clearly stepped foot in town. This is a map of Mirror Lake. Here's where Jane's body was found. Here's where Mina and I found the puddle of her blood. These are the few areas I could think of where a vampire might hide out." Eli pointed to circles on the map he'd created. "I think we should split up. A few of us should talk with the Montevallos while others search for this vampire's, or vampires', hideout. Who wants to do what?"

"Maybe it would be best if you talked to the Montevallos first," Charles insisted. "It might be best to gain as much knowledge on the subject before diving in headfirst."

"Sounds good," Dorian agreed with his dad.

Eli's jaw twitched as he contemplated the suggestion.

"All right," he said. "After we talk to them, we'll talk to the witches, and then we'll split up and search the town."

Murmurs of agreement were spoken. We would talk to the Montevallos and then the Caraways, afterward I'd make sure Eli ate something and got some rest. He needed both. Especially if we were going up against the Midnight Reaper anytime soon.

14

The Montevallo vampires lived near the edge of town in an old brick mansion. It consisted of two massive stories with a high-pitched A-framed roof. There was a circular gravel driveway in the front and a perfectly manicured yard. A small house sat to the right of the mansion made from the same materials. I assumed it was the caretaker's home. Did they have a caretaker? I imagined they had to have someone to care for the place while they were away for years on end.

Did this caretaker know he worked for vampires? Or was he compelled to not notice strange happenings by Ivette?

My stomach soured as thoughts of the doctors Regina had compelled filled my mind. They'd been practically zombies. I hoped that wasn't the case with the Montevallos' caretaker.

As we crept up the gravel road, I spotted the same baby blue car I witnessed Julian drive. Two more vehicles were parked in front of it—a cherry red sports car and a solid black one. Both were different models and brands. I assumed they belonged to Julian's sisters.

Wasn't there a fourth sibling? Another male?

When would he be making an appearance in Mirror Lake? Did he even get along with his siblings? Was he returning home like they had? Maybe he didn't want to.

I didn't blame him.

If I were a vampire, I wasn't sure I'd return home either. What was the point? Everyone you knew and loved would have already passed. It seemed too depressing.

Instead, I'd travel the world, never staying in one place long.

And unlike the vampires in the paranormal shows Gracie watched, I'd stay away from New Orleans. Gran had taken me and Gracie once a couple years ago when she paid a well-known witch who owned a shop on Bourbon Street a visit for some special herb seeds. That section of the city could be pretty disgusting. Even in the middle of the day, it still smelled like puke.

Eli cut the engine of his truck and let out a long exhale. It was clear he didn't want to be here.

"This place is a hell of a lot bigger than I thought it would be," Dorian insisted as he slipped out the passenger seat and glanced up, soaking in the mansion. "I can't believe I've never scoped this place out before."

"I know what you mean," I muttered as climbed out of the truck behind him. I slammed the passenger door shut and started toward the front door. An intricate vine with flowers had been carved out of the wood door that nearly took my breath away.

I hadn't stepped foot inside yet and already I was wowed by the place's beauty.

"It's too big for me," Eli growled as he walked straight to the front door.

"I think it's amazing," I said. "There's this romantic vibe oozing from it I like."

"Romantic vibe?" Dorian teased. "God, you're such a damn girl sometimes."

I rolled my eyes, but before I could say anything in response to his jab, the front door of the place opened.

Julian stood in the threshold, dressed in dark jeans and a gray cable knit sweater. His dark-framed glasses reflected the sunlight behind us, and his hair had been spiked to perfection again. I wondered how much time it took him to get it to stand up like that each morning.

My gaze drifted to his face. The expression he wore had my wolf on guard.

He didn't seem happy to see us. In fact, he looked on edge. Anxiety and tension rippled off him, vibrating through the air and making me question if coming here was a good idea. I glanced at the guys, trying to gauge their reaction. Dorian seemed uneasy, but Eli looked as though he was ready to go head-to-head with Julian in a full-out brawl.

"Julian," Eli said with a sharp edge to his tone. "We have something we need to discuss with you. It involves the Midnight Reaper."

I reached out for Eli's hand and smoothed my thumb against the length of his index finger to calm him. Where was all of his tension and hostility coming from? Was it because he was in the presence of a vampire? Even though this wasn't the one responsible for his father's death, his wolf might not care—which meant his wolf might be fighting him for control or fueling him with rage.

The twitch under Eli's eye seemed to diminish at the same time his features visibly relaxed. My touch was having the effect on him I'd wanted. This was good. He needed to get his crap together because Julian wasn't the enemy—the Midnight Reaper was.

At the same time Eli seemed to relax from my touch, Julian relaxed as well.

"I had a feeling you'd be by soon," he said as he stepped aside and motioned for us to enter. "Please, come in."

He'd had a feeling we'd be coming by soon? What did that mean? Did Julian have the power of premonition? His youngest sister could compel people, and I knew he had a talent. I just didn't know what. It had to do with the mind or possibly emotions, I was positive of it.

My gaze narrowed on him as I walked past him into the mansion he called home.

Gleaming cherrywood floors and dark paneled walls captured my attention. There was a massive crystal chandelier casting light from behind us in every direction. It looked like a gigantic diamond dripping from the ceiling.

Julian closed the door behind us once we were all inside. He moved down the richly colored wooden steps that led to a sunken great room next, motioning we follow.

A rich color palette of reds, creams, and deep browns decorated the room. It was all too dark and dreary for my tastes, but this was the home of vampires.

Julian continued to a chocolate brown sofa positioned in front of the stone fireplace and situated himself there.

"Please, have a seat," he said. "Can I get anyone anything to drink?"

"No," Eli insisted as he released my hand to sit on the opposite sofa. The tension was back in his features.

Dorian sat beside him. "Nope, I'm good."

Julian's eyes locked on me. I shook my head.

"Okay," Julian said. "You mentioned the Midnight Reaper. What about him brings you to me?"

"Are you aware of his killings?" Eli asked. His facial features tightened as he spoke. This was more difficult for him than I'd thought it would be.

Julian nodded. "Yes, unfortunately."

"Are you aware the killer has struck in Mirror Lake within the last twenty-four hours?" Eli pressed.

Julian eyed Eli carefully. "I am, but I'm sorry, I'm not sure where you're going with this. My sisters and I heard about the death of a young girl, but why would that bring you to my doorstep?"

"Jane, her name was Jane," Eli insisted. "She was killed by the Midnight Reaper. So was my father."

Julian's brows pinched together. "I'm sorry; I had no idea. My condolences."

Eli nodded.

"We're here because we aren't sure whether the Midnight Reaper is one vampire or multiple," Dorian said when Eli seemed to have gone quiet. I reached out for Eli's hand again. This time, my touch didn't seem to have the same effect as before. Maybe he was too far gone in his memories of finding his father. "We think he, or they, might have a special power as well," Dorian continued.

"What sort of power?" Julian asked as something more than curiosity built in his eyes.

"Have you ever come across a vampire who happens to be exceptionally fast?" Dorian asked.

Julian leaned back. "Yes, actually I have. A few in my time, to be honest."

"Is it a popular power among vampires?" Dorian pressed.

"Yes." There was a smugness to Julian's tone I didn't care for. "All vampires have this ability, but some are faster than others. Same with humans. Not everyone's top speed is the same."

"What about vampires who can make you see things that aren't there?" I asked.

Julian grew stiff. Clearly, he hadn't been expecting my question. I had his attention though.

High heels clicking across the wood floor echoed close by. A woman slightly older than Julian stepped into the room with us. She wore a black leather dress that hit above her knees and a pair of strappy stilettos. Her dark hair was twisted on top of her head into a formal bun, and her lips were painted blood red. She held a wineglass filled with a deep red liquid I wanted to think of as wine but knew it was most likely blood.

"Let me introduce you to my oldest sister, Octavia," Julian said once she situated herself on the sofa beside him and placed her glass on the coffee table. "Sister, this is Eli, Mina, and—I'm sorry, but I don't know your name," he said as he pointed to Dorian.

"Dorian," Dorian introduced himself.

"And Dorian of the Mirror Lake wolves," Julian insisted, finishing his introductions.

"I know they're of the Mirror Lake wolves. Any idiot could sense that," Octavia said in a raspy tone. She crossed her long, slender legs. "What exactly are they doing here? Do they need our help again?"

"No," Eli said in an eerily calm and authority-ridden voice. "Quite the contrary. We came to warn you the Midnight Reaper is now in Mirror Lake."

"And why would you need to warn us?" Octavia asked as her dark eyes drifted over the length of Eli.

I wasn't sure if she was sizing him up because she liked the look of him, or because she was annoyed with him. Either way, I was beginning to think Octavia Montevallo was a grade A bitch.

"Because when my father was murdered by him last night, there was a message written in blood across his forearm," Eli snapped. Clearly, he didn't like the tone she was using with him.

Julian shifted and something passed over his face. The same emotion seemed to register in Octavia's eyes for a split-second as well. It caused my wolf to sit up and take notice. The fine hairs along the back of my neck stood on end.

The Montevallo vampires were hiding something. The question was: What?

"What was the message?" Julian asked.

"One down," Eli seethed.

I squeezed his hand in mine as silence bloomed through the room. His rage was sweeping off him in waves. I knew the vampires could sense it as plainly as Dorian and I could, and I didn't want this situation to get out of hand. No one needed to feel threatened here. We were just talking.

"That could mean anything. Why waste your time warning us?" Octavia asked as she glared at her fingernails.

"Because we aren't sure what it means," I said, finally deciding to speak up. "We know it can mean one of two things—either this killer vampire is hell-bent on wiping out our pack members one by one, or he's planning to go after all supernaturals in town. In which case, we decided to warn you. You're welcome."

My flippant attitude garnered her attention. She lifted her dark eyes to lock with mine, and I swore I saw the flicker of a smile twist the corners of her red painted lips.

"Also, we'd like to know the best way to take out a speedster vampire," Dorian insisted. "If that's what we're dealing with."

"Thank you for your warning. We appreciate you taking the time to give it to us personally," Julian insisted. Octavia had gone back to picking at her nails. While she was the oldest Montevallo sibling out of the vampires I'd met so far, Julian appeared to run things. Maybe he was the first created? After all, with vampires human age didn't count. "However, there is no trick to take down a speedster. They're the same as any vampire."

"What about one who can make others see things that aren't there?" I asked, reminding them all of the other power we seemed to have encountered with the Midnight Reaper.

"I'm afraid I can't give you an answer for that either," Julian insisted.

I waited for him to elaborate, but he never did. In fact, he didn't seem to want to discuss the issue further.

"Okay, well. I think we're done here." Eli stood. "We'll be paying the Caraway witches a visit next to warn them as well, and then we'll begin patrols."

"Patrols?" Julian repeated.

"We have to find the Midnight Reaper, whether it's one vampire or more. The safety of my pack and the town of Mirror Lake relies on it," Eli insisted.

Even though he didn't say it, it was clear Eli was hell-bent on getting revenge too. I could taste his desire for it in the air.

"I'd like to help with patrolling if you'll allow me," Julian surprised me by saying.

I waited for Octavia to offer her help as well, but she didn't. Instead, she reached for her wineglass. It slid across the table directly to her hand. I blinked. Apparently, Octavia could move things with her mind. It seemed as though each Montevallo had a special power.

"Absolutely," Eli said. "We'll always welcome more help. Meet me at my trailer at seven o'clock tonight. I'll give you your designated search area."

Seven tonight? I was surprised Eli had said such a late time, considering it was almost 10 a.m. Maybe he was finally realizing he needed sleep and food to fuel him if he wanted to make it through the search tonight and hold his own.

"I'll be there," Julian insisted as he walked us to the door.

The three of us followed him. I could feel Octavia's eyes on us. While I didn't think the woman was evil, I did think she had an attitude from hell. I also thought she and her brother were hiding something. They knew something about the Midnight Reaper but were refusing to tell us. Why?

15

We pulled into the gravel parking lot beside the Caraway Inn. It was also another massive house. Four stories, including the attic level, towered above us as we climbed out of Eli's truck. A set of brown stone steps led up to a screened-in porch that ran the entire length of the house. The white exterior with brown accents gave the inn a homey feel. An array of beautiful flowers in a multitude of colors and multiple forms of greenery landscaped the place magnifying the warm, comfortable vibe emanating from the place.

Knowing it was inhabited by witches had me questioning if the vibes coming off it were the result of one of the Caraways' powers or a spell. One that made the inn seem more inviting.

"Hanging out in these gigantic mansions today is going to make returning home to my little trailer feel cruddy," Dorian muttered as we started up the stone steps to the front door.

Rowena Caraway opened the door before any of us had a chance to knock. Back at Julian's, I knew his swiftness to open the door had most likely been because of his vampire hearing; here, I attributed it to the powers Rowena was said to possess. She often seemed to have a knack for knowing things.

My gaze drifted over her, taking in her casual gray slacks and a lightweight black sweater. Her dark hair fell to her chin in sleek strands, and her chocolate brown eyes appeared warm and inviting, same as the smile spread on her face at the sight of us.

"Hello," she said and then motioned for us to step inside. "It's a surprise to see the three of you here. I would say I hope all is well, but I can tell from your auras it's not." Her dark brows knitted together as she continued to stare at us.

A flowery scent filled the foyer of the inn as I stepped inside. I glanced around as the realization I'd lived in Mirror Lake my entire life and had yet to step foot inside the Caraway Inn rushed through me. Ridley and I were friends, but I never visited her at home. Same way she never did me. Enjoying the peace and serenity oozing through the place, I made a note to remedy that.

Gray walls with white trim and weathered wood floors made up the foyer. What little bit of furniture filled the tight space was black. A staircase stood ahead. The place was not at all gaudy or outdated like I'd thought it would be. In fact, it was clean and classic, modern even yet still charming and welcoming.

"Why don't the three of you follow me? I'll whip up some tea while you fill me in on what it is you're here for," Rowena said.

We followed Rowena into the kitchen where a large bay window filled with plants resting on rustic wood shelves captured my eye. A broad wooden table sat a few feet away with mismatched chairs spaced sporadically around. Its surface was covered with glass jars of dried herbs that had me thinking of Gran. She would love this place. Why didn't she visit Rowena? They clearly had something in common.

Unless these were magical herbs, ones only usable by a witch.

I glanced at the rest of the room. Herbs in various stages of drying hung from a rack near the stove. White cabinets and butterscotch-colored butcher block counter-tops gleamed in the can lights of the high ceiling.

"Please, have a seat," Rowena insisted. She pointed to the bar stools tucked underneath the island countertop.

"Thanks," Eli said as he pulled one out for me. I eyed him as I situated myself. He was calm. Too calm. Especially with the way his behavior had been at the Monte-vallos. "And you're right, we aren't here bringing good news."

Even as he spoke, the sense of calmness lingered around him. Was there a spell responsible? Or was it something stemming from Rowena?

"I'm sorry we're coming over unannounced, but this is an important matter. One I didn't feel should be discussed over the phone." Eli placed his hands on the counter as he watched Rowena fill three mugs with boiling water from a kettle on the stove.

Had she been expecting us, or did she always have a kettle of water ready for her guests staying at the inn? It was hard to tell.

"I understand," Rowena said as she scooped two spoonfuls of dried herbs from a glass jar labeled *calm and comfort* into three loose leaf tea holders. I watched as she plopped them into the steaming mugs of water next.

"I know you're aware of the Midnight Reaper killings. Mina spoke to Ridley yesterday about them. Ridley claimed you had plans to put up a ward around Mirror Lake in an effort to keep any vampire who wasn't part of the Montevallo family out," Eli said.

Rowena nodded. "That's true."

"Would this ward of yours still work if the vampire, or vampires, making up the Midnight Reaper were already in Mirror Lake?" Dorian asked.

Rowena passed us each a mug. Her lips pinched together into a frown before she spoke. "I'm aware the Midnight Reaper is already in town. Ridley told me about the young girl stumbling into the trailer park last night. Such a tragedy. I can't imagine what her family must be going through." She took a sip of her tea and stared into space for a long moment before shifting her attention back to the three of us and the question Dorian had asked. "I do believe even if the vampire, or vampires, were within the town limits, the ward would still work. Theoretically, it would cast them out the instant it went up."

"When will you be able to put one in place?" Eli asked.

"Unfortunately, I can't set the ward in place until the full moon, which, as you know, is two nights away," Rowena said.

"Is there a way to bypass the full moon? The Midnight Reaper is dangerous. Not only did he attack and kill Jane Hawker but also my father." Eli's voice was low when he spoke. I reached for his hand, hoping my touch would bring him comfort again. It couldn't be any easier to say this time around than it had the previous times.

"Oh no. I'm so sorry." Rowena's gaze fixed on Eli. Genuine concern reflected in her eyes. "Please, let me know if there's anything I can do for you or your family. Your pack." Rowena's voice shook when she spoke and tears pooled in her eyes.

While I knew the werewolves and the witches weren't chummy with one another, Rowena had still known our alpha well. They'd been friends, for lack of a better word.

"Thank you," Eli insisted. "Unfortunately, letting you know of my father's passing isn't the only reason I'm here. I wanted to warn you the Midnight Reaper left a message on my father's forearm. It said *one down*. Because we aren't certain it means this vampire, or group of them, is targeting our pack members specifically or if they're targeting all supernaturals in Mirror Lake, we wanted to give you a heads up."

Eli's steadiness surprised me. While I'd always been impressed with the way he handled himself in such a businesslike manner during tough situations, this one was for the record books.

Maybe there was something more to the tea Rowena had given us. Was it possible it added another layer of whatever comfort spell rang between these walls?

No wonder this place was always filled with guests.

I took a tentative sip to test the tea out on myself since my nerves were frazzled. Warmth rushed through me, but I couldn't be sure there was anything magical about the sensation.

"I truly appreciate you taking the time to warn me," Rowena insisted.

"You're welcome." Eli nodded. "We're beginning patrols in an effort to catch this killer before anyone else is harmed."

"Wonderful. I hope you're able to find whoever's responsible and bring them to justice properly," Rowena said with a coldness I'd never heard from her before. "If not, then at the very least, I hope they don't hurt anyone else between now and the full moon so my ward can cast them out of town for good."

While I wanted the Midnight Reaper out of town as much as the next person, I didn't think casting him out so he could continue to wreak havoc on the rest of the world was the best solution.

"I think we're all wishing for something similar," Eli insisted. He took a sip of tea, and I noticed him relax even more.

"Before you go, would you like me to pour your tea into a to-go cup?" Rowena asked.

"Sure. That would be great," I said. Her calming tea

was probably the only way I was going to get Eli to relax enough to catch some shut-eye before beginning his patrol tonight. "Thanks."

"You're welcome." Rowena reached for our mugs and then poured the contents into standard to-go cups you'd find at a coffee shop. "Please come back and see me should you need anything else. I'll also be in contact after the full moon to keep you posted on whether the ward went up successfully."

Eli nodded as he stood and reached for one of the cups she was passing out. "We'll talk soon for sure."

Rowena walked us to the front door of the inn.

"Oh, tell Ridley I said hey," I said as I paused in the foyer.

"I will." She winked. "She's out with Benji at the moment."

"Figures." I grinned.

After the three of us situated ourselves inside the cab of Eli's truck, I took another sip of tea. My muscles loosened as my mind cleared. Whatever was in the stuff reminded me of Gran's calming tea except this was more potent. Like times a hundred.

Of course, I'd never tell Gran that. She'd kick my butt for comparing her natural home remedy to a witch's brew that was destined to be more powerful.

"I feel better," Dorian insisted as Eli cranked the engine of his truck and pulled away from Caraway Inn.

"Of course you do." I laughed. "It's the tea."

"Well, yeah." Dorian grinned as he took another sip. "But not entirely because of that. I feel better because we talked to the supernaturals in town. We're all on the same page, and planning to do our part to rid Mirror Lake of this evil. Teamwork. It's a beautiful thing."

He was right. Knowing we had help from the vampires and witches made me feel more at ease as well. Maybe we could defeat whatever we were up against without losing anyone else to its darkness.

I leaned back against the bench seat of Eli's truck and sipped my tea, letting its soothing properties work its magic.

16

When we pulled into the trailer park, Eli looked exhausted. I reached out and rubbed his back when he leaned forward to rest against the steering wheel.

"Maybe you should head inside and get some rest," I suggested in a soft voice, hoping he wouldn't fight me.

"I can't. We need to focus on patrolling. I know I said I'd deal with that all later tonight, but I feel like it needs to be handled now," he said. "More rotations need to be set in place. I need to be out there helping."

"I think Mina is right," Dorian chimed in from where he sat beside me. "I think it would do you good to get some sleep first. I can handle all of that while you rest."

Eli didn't speak. Instead, his jaw worked back and forth while he seemed to be contemplating what to say.

"You're not doing anyone any favors by being exhausted and rundown. We're hoping to catch the Midnight Reaper," Dorian insisted, pressing harder on the subject. I was grateful it was coming from him and not me. I didn't want to sound as though I was nagging. "Which means you're going to need every bit of strength you have to help take the bastard down."

"Yeah, okay." Eli pulled the keys from the ignition and popped his driver door open. "Follow me inside. I'll set you up with the map. It's already sectioned off; you just need to assign sections to people."

Eli slipped out of the truck, and Dorian and I followed behind him to the trailer. Gifts of condolences from the pack littered the wooden steps of our place. The sight had love for my pack rushing through me. My wolf even let out a howl of approval for their generosity and compassion.

"You should eat something too," I said as I reached to pick up a casserole dish covered with aluminum foil. "The pack has made sure we have a variety of things to choose from. Better not let it all go to waste."

"That dish looks familiar." Dorian stepped closer. "I bet that's Sheila's tuna casserole. God, I love that stuff. Care if I get a little bowl of it before I leave?"

I frowned at him at the same time Eli said he could take the whole thing if he wanted.

"What? Don't like tuna?" Dorian asked him, purposely ignoring the look I flashed his way.

Where were his manners? It was rude to ask for any of the food. He wasn't the one who'd lost his father.

"I like tuna," Eli said as he opened the door of our trailer as wide as the gifts and food would allow. "I just know I won't eat it. I'm not hungry."

My heart dropped. I hated seeing him this way, so

hollowed-out and heartbroken, knowing I could do nothing to make him feel better.

"I know you probably have no appetite," I said as I crossed to the kitchen and set the casserole dish and a few more gifts I'd picked up on my way up the stairs onto the counter. "But sleep isn't the only thing your body needs. It also needs food, even if it's something small."

Eli grabbed a lemon bar from one of the plates I'd brought in. He put it to his lips and took a massive bite, his eyes never wavering from me. I knew he was being spiteful, but I was too happy to see him eat something, even a sugary something, to care.

"The map is over here." He moved to the living room where the maps were still sprawled out on the coffee table. "Like I said, the sections are already marked for the most part. You just need to assign a couple people to each."

"Will do," Dorian said as he took the map from Eli and then made his way to the door. "You get some rest. I'll be back at seven with a fresh crew to rotate out."

"Sounds good. Thanks," Eli said as he slouched down on the couch.

He propped his feet up on the coffee table and finished off the lemon bar. I stepped to Moonshine's crate and gathered her up so I could take her outside. She spotted Eli on the couch, but I refused to let her down.

When I stepped outside, I spotted Felicia walking toward Eli's mom's trailer with a huge Tupperware dish in her hands. My heart skipped a few beats as I remembered I had yet to pay Eli's mom a visit. I hadn't even brought her the customary gift or paid my respects yet.

I made a mental note to do so after Eli fell asleep.

By the time Moonshine finished her business, Eli was passed out on the couch. A small smile quirked at the corners of my lips as I listened to him snore while I placed Moonshine back in her crate.

"Thank you, Rowena, for your special tea," I muttered. "It worked like a charm."

I cleaned up the kitchen by placing the perishable things our pack members had brought into the fridge and arranging the rest on the counter. A bouquet of white roses stood out to me. They were stunning and seemed to be the perfect gift for Eli's mom. Still, I felt I needed something else. I grabbed a glass jar of calming loose leaf tea from the emergency kit Gran had made for us and decided that should be enough.

My heart thundered in my chest as I let myself out of the trailer and made my way to Eli's parents.

The front steps of Eli's parents' place were more decorated than ours had been. This was to be expected though. After all, Wesley had been our alpha.

I sidestepped a couple vases of flowers as I made my way up the stairs to the door and knocked. When no one answered, I knocked again.

"June, it's Mina. I wanted to see how you're doing," I shouted through the metal door, hoping when she heard it was me she'd let me in. It was clear she hadn't answered the door for anyone else who'd come by.

"Come in," June shouted from somewhere inside. I steeled myself as I gripped the doorknob, ready to face a heartbroken woman who was normally happy.

"Hi," I said as I stepped inside the dimly lit trailer.

June was on the couch, still in her pajamas. "I brought you flowers and some of Gran's special tea. Would you like me to make you a mug?"

June's bright green eyes that were so eerily similar to Eli's focused on me. "How is he?"

"He's doing the best he can," I said, knowing whom she was talking about.

"Has the filthy vampire responsible been found yet?" she asked.

Movement from the back of the trailer captured my attention. My gaze drifted through the kitchen to the hallway where I spotted Eli's youngest brother, Jonas, eavesdropping on our conversation.

"No." I hated the word with a fiery passion as it slipped past my lips because I knew it wouldn't bring her the sense of satisfaction she was hoping for. "Not yet. There's a plan in motion, though. We'll find the vampire and bring him to justice. Don't worry."

My voice was strong. I could feel my determination pulsating through my words. They gave me strength, and I hoped they did the same for her and Jonas as well.

"I don't doubt you, Mina," June insisted as she shifted around on the couch. She smoothed her hair away from her face, and wiped her nose with the back of her hand. "He's ready for this, you know. As scared he might seem to take over, Eli's been ready for a long time."

"I know."

"Wesley groomed him properly for the role, even if he was unwilling to let go of his position in authority," June said. "Eli's going to make a great alpha. He's going to make Wesley proud. I know it."

Her words brought tears to my eyes. I had to find something to busy myself with, if not I was at risk of breaking down. I couldn't cry. Not here. Not in front of June or Jonas. This was their moment to grieve, not mine.

I crossed to the kitchen where I placed the vase of flowers on the counter and then rummaged through the cabinets for a coffee mug. Once I found one, I filled it with tap water and popped it in the microwave.

"I'm so glad he has you. I can't be there for him like I should through this. I can't be there for any of my boys like I should right now," June said, surprising me. "Not when I feel like I can't breathe."

The heartache reflected in her words had me shifting to look at her. Tears streamed down her face, and one of her hands came to rest over her heart. I swallowed hard. The threat of tears pierced my eyes and stung the back of my throat.

"There's a huge hole in place of where my heart used to be, and I'm drowning in the blackness of it. I can't breathe, Mina, because he's gone," she sobbed.

The timer on the microwave went off, and I stood there at a complete loss for words. There was nothing I could say to take away even an ounce of her pain.

After a few seconds passed, I wiped my nose on the back of my hand and pulled the warm mug of water from the microwave. Next, I reached for Gran's tea.

"Your tea is ready," I whispered as I made my way back to her.

The desire to say I was sorry, to offer some form of condolence, built inside me but nothing passed from my lips. It didn't matter because anything I said would only fall on deaf ears. June looked as though she wasn't here with me. She looked as though she were somewhere else far away and submerged in her own pain and sorrow.

"Your tea," I said as I held the mug out to her.

June's hands reached out to grab it without ever looking at me.

Was she lost in the memories of her husband?

A sharp pain stabbed at my heart. I couldn't imagine living without Eli. Never being able to wake up beside him again. Never being able to hear him say my name or to whisper I love you in the middle of the night to each other before we fell asleep.

"We were together for thirty-seven years," June whispered over the rim of her mug. Tears spilled from her eyes, landing in her tea. "I thought we had more time together. How am I supposed to continue on without him? What am I supposed to do now?"

I placed a hand on hers and moved to sit on the couch beside her. "Live. It's what he would want you to do."

Somehow I knew that was what Wesley Vargas, our alpha, would've wanted me to say to her.

"He would have wanted you to continue on with your life. To see things. To experience things. To be there for your children. He wouldn't have wanted you to be swallowed up by the darkness of that black hole and never break the surface to the light again," I said.

My words touched June. I knew this when her lips twisted into a tiny grin as she wiped her nose with the back of her hand.

"That's exactly what Wesley would say to me if he were here," she whispered. "Thank you."

"You're welcome," I said as I stood. "Sip your tea. I'm going to bring in the gifts the pack left you outside."

"I feel bad for ignoring everyone. I just couldn't bring myself to face anyone yet," June said.

I twisted the knob and opened the door. "It's okay. I'm sure they understand."

I stepped outside and carried in all of the goodies from the pack. There were loads of flowers, trinkets, and dishes of food.

One thing was certain, our alpha had been loved.

My sense of wonder shifted to sadness and then anger as thoughts of the vampire responsible for taking away someone so precious to us all floated through my mind. Determination to find the Midnight Reaper and seek revenge heated my blood as I carried in the final items the pack had left for June and the boys.

I spread the flowers around the trailer and placed the food in the fridge. I left the trinkets and gifts on the dining room table, hoping if June didn't go through them that one of the boys would.

Once I was finished, I said goodbye and let myself out. A breeze kicked up as I started down the steps of the trailer, sending leaves fluttering around me. For a split-second, I found myself thinking it was the spirit of our alpha thanking me for having brought a small sense of comfort to his wife.

Maybe it was silly, but I couldn't help myself.

I took a few steps away from the trailer, and then paused to soak in the warmth and love I felt at the memory of the only alpha I'd ever known. The front door of June's trailer opened, pulling me out of my thoughts.

Jonas was creeping down the stairs. I started to say something to him but clamped my mouth shut when I saw him scoop up a backpack off the ground from beneath his bedroom window. He hoisted it onto his back and looked around as though he were up to no good. When his eyes landed on me, he froze.

"Hey, Jonas," I said. "What's up?"

"Nothing."

"Nothing? You sure about that? It looks like you're in a hurry to get somewhere," I said as I stepped toward him.

He remained where he was as though his little feet were rooted into the ground, even when I reached around him and unzipped his backpack to glance inside. The contents didn't surprise me. It was clear from how sneaky he was trying to be he was attempting to run away.

"Lots of food. A couple of changes of clothes," I said as I released his backpack and struggled to get him to make eye contact with me. "Are you running away?" My words came out angrier than necessary, but it was only because I couldn't believe he was bailing on his family during a time like this.

What the hell was going through his mind?

"No," Jonas bit out.

"Really? Because it looks like it."

"I'm not," he insisted as his eyes lifted to meet with mine. "I wouldn't do that. Especially not now."

"Then what are you doing?" I asked. "Because it sure seems to me you've got all the supplies to runaway crammed in there."

"I'm not running away, okay?" he snapped. "I'm

going to get the vampire who took my dad from me and made my mom so sad."

All the air left my lungs.

My heart, though already fragile from everything that had transpired, broke into a million tiny pieces as I stared into Jonas's tear-filled eyes.

What could I say to a little boy standing before me, ready to take on the monster who'd taken so much from him in such a short span of time and brought the most pain and heartache he'd ever witnessed to everyone he loved?

"You have to let me go. I need to go after him," Jonas pleaded. "Please don't try to stop me. I have to do this. For my mom. I heard you say the vampire hasn't been caught yet. Nobody's got him, but I will. I'll get him, and when I do, I'll kill him for what he's done."

I stared at Jonas. He was nine years old, but his conviction and determination were as strong as my own. As strong as Eli's.

"Jonas." My teeth sank into my bottom lip as I shook my head. "You can't go after him. Your mom needs you too much."

It was all I could think to say. The only reason I could give that might make him stay.

"I know she needs me," he insisted as his hands fisted at his sides. "She needs me to kill this vampire."

"No. She needs you to be with her through this tough time. Most of all, she needs you to stay safe," I said, hoping he'd wise up and see reason.

"You think I'm too young," Jonas spat. "You think I can't stop the vampire who took my dad from me, but you don't know. You don't know what I'm capable of. You don't know how I feel."

He sounded so grown-up. An angry man trapped inside a little boy.

I knew that wasn't the case though. At the end of the day, Jonas Vargas was still just a child.

"You're right. I don't know how you feel, but I do know what you're capable of. You're capable of great things, Jonas. That's why you need to be here for your mom. For your brothers. For your pack," I insisted. "There's a plan in motion to take out the vampire responsible for your father's death. Your brother has a lot of members from the pack working on it. Not even just them, he's also got the Caraway witches and the Montevallo vampires helping too. Please, trust me when I say the vampire responsible for causing you and your mom pain will be brought to justice," I said as I got down to his level and pulled him in for a hug.

He broke down in my arms. Sobs spurred from somewhere deep within him as his tears flowed like a twin rivers from his eyes, soaking through my shirt. I didn't let him go. Instead, I let him cry until he could cry no more, and then I zipped up his backpack and told him to head inside and sit with his mom because she could really use some love from him right now.

Miraculously, Jonas wiped his face and did as I said. The instant he disappeared inside the trailer, someone cleared their throat behind me. Micha, the middle Vargas boy, stood a few feet away. His hands were shoved in his pockets and tears stained his cheeks.

"Thanks for talking to some sense into him," Micha said without looking at me.

"No problem. You're going to have to watch him, though."

Micha's bright green eyes lifted to lock with mine as his brows furrowed. "Why do you say that?"

"Because, he's stubborn and strong-headed like all of you Vargas boys. This won't be the last time he tries to go after the vampire himself. I talked him down, but what I said won't stick with him for long. He's going to need you to remind him to let Eli and the others take care of this on their own, especially if the vampire isn't taken out quickly."

"You're right." Micha sighed. "I guess."

He hurried past me and slipped inside the trailer without a glance back.

I let out a breath of air and tucked a few stray strands of hair behind my ear before I started toward home. I hoped Eli was still sleeping because all I wanted to do was curl up beside him and take a nap myself in preparation for the crazy night ahead of us.

17

"These are the areas left for us to search." Dorian pointed to four sections on the map, then shifted his attention to another area. "This is the section we searched today. No one reported any findings that might relate to the Midnight Reaper."

"Could that mean the vampire, or group of vampires, has moved on from Mirror Lake already?" I asked. It was a long shot, considering the messages left behind on both victims we'd seen him take since being in town.

"Doubtful," Eli snapped.

I knew his tone and what he'd said wasn't an intentional jab at me, but his attitude was starting to get to me. His mood was continuously sour.

I swallowed hard. This wasn't the Eli I knew, but this was the Eli standing before me. He was hurting. I had to cut him slack because of it.

This meant biting my tongue. A lot.

"Unfortunately, I think it means whoever is doing

this has decided to lie low," Dorian said. "Maybe they're watching us. Maybe not. Whatever the reason for us having not found them yet is of no matter because we will find them, and when we do we will make them pay."

The level of certainty and determination echoing through Dorian's words vibrated through the trailer. Julian even seemed to squirm from the intensity. Or was he squirming because of something else?

My mind circled back to when we paid him a visit at home; I'd thought him and his sister, Octavia, were hiding something. I watched him as Dorian spoke. He seemed uncomfortable, but not enough for me to think he was the Midnight Reaper.

However, that didn't mean he didn't know who he was.

"I've already told the others to take a few hours to rest," Dorian said, pulling my attention back to the here and now. "Once they've slept for a little while and gotten something to eat, they're going to resume patrolling with the rest of us."

"Sounds good." Eli wasted no time folding up the map on the coffee table. "We should head out. Get a jump on the search."

Chatter erupted around me as everyone discussed who they should pair up with. I scooped Moonshine up from where she slept curled into my side on the couch and started for the door. There was no telling how long I'd be gone tonight, but I knew Eli would be out all night. It was best to take her out now before putting her in her crate.

"Earlier, we split into teams of three," Dorian said as I

leaned around him to grab Moonshine's leash off the counter. "Eli wanted you paired up with Violet tonight," he insisted.

"Yeah, I talked to her earlier today about it. She's glad we invited her to help," I said as I fumbled with Moonshine's leash. "She's supposed to meet me in a few minutes."

"Good." Dorian nodded. "Julian finishes off the rest of your group."

I glanced at Eli. Apparently, he hadn't said he wanted to be paired with me and Violet. This hurt. Distance was building between us I didn't care for.

As though he could feel my eyes on him, Eli glanced at me from across the room.

"Why did you put Julian with me and Violet instead of yourself?" I asked him point blank.

"Because you'll be safer with him," Eli insisted.

His words were like a physical blow. What the hell did that mean?

"Safer how?" I didn't understand.

Eli crossed to where I stood. "Mina, please understand," he said, clearly able to sense how put out with his decision I was. "I couldn't get to my dad in time, and the last thing I want is to not be able to get to you in time either. I'd much rather you hung out here instead of patrolling, but I know that's not an option. Not for you." A slight smile quirked at the corners of his lips. "I know you well enough to know you prefer being in the thick of things. You're strong, and you're stubborn. Neither of those are characteristics I want stamped out of you. I enjoy them. So, I'm compromising," he said as he licked his lips and then cupped my face between his warm palms to stare me directly in the eyes. "If you're going to come searching tonight, I want you paired with Julian. He's strong. He's powerful. And he'd be a good match for this vampire, considering he is one. While I hate the thought of not having you in my sight, I think you're safest with him."

I didn't know what to say.

"I'll take good care of her," Julian insisted.

Eli kissed me and then walked away. I realized then it wasn't the loss of his father tearing him up, but also the potential threat of losing me the same way.

I opened the front door and stepped outside, taking Moonshine with me. Eli wanted me safe. I wouldn't be judgmental. I understood, now that he'd taken a second to explain where his head was at with me.

Movement at the edge of the woods captured my attention. The pack members who were waiting to go on patrol stood there. My heartbeat kicked up a notch as I thought of how much bloodshed could potentially occur tonight. The Midnight Reaper was dangerous. I knew this and so did my wolf, which was why there was a part of me that felt like we were going off to war.

I sent a silent prayer up to the goddess of the moon, asking that she protect us all tonight and every night after until the Midnight Reaper was captured.

Once Moonshine did her business, I took her back inside. I locked her in her crate and said goodnight before I pulled the towel down to block her vision.

I stepped to Eli's side and placed a kiss on his cheek. "The others are waiting near the woods."

"Okay, it's time to go," Eli insisted. His arm snaked around my waist and pulled me in close to him. "Good luck out there tonight, everyone. Be safe. Let's find this bastard and bring him to justice before he has a chance to hurt anyone else."

A collective round of shouts and applause sounded through the trailer. We all stepped out into the night to search our designated areas and hopefully find the monster lurking somewhere in Mirror Lake.

———

I WALKED between Julian and Violet as we patrolled our section of the woods together.

"You don't have to be here, you know," Julian insisted as he glanced at Violet. "We can walk you back and resume our search without you if this is too much for you to handle."

Violet folded her arms around her midsection but refused to meet his gaze. "I'm fine."

"Okay." Julian smirked. "I just wanted to let you know, to give you an out if you wanted it."

Violet glanced at me from the corner of her eye.

"I don't need an out," she said, but even I could hear the tremor in her voice.

She looked terrified. Had Julian been able to look at her and sense her fear the same as I could, or was he tapping into what she was feeling on a deeper level? What was his power? Was he a mind reader? It wasn't the first time I'd thought such a thing.

"I wasn't trying to upset you," Julian said to Violet

before he shifted his attention to me. "Can you stop being so skeptical of me? I'm only here to help."

My heart skipped a beat. Was he in my head, or feeling what I was? I wasn't sure I cared for either. Thoughts and feelings were private. He was being intrusive.

"Then you need to tell me more about yourself," I insisted, refusing to look away from him as I stepped over a fallen branch.

The ghost of a smile quirked at the corners of his lips as he adjusted his glasses. "What would you like to know?"

"What power you have," I said without beating around the bush. "I know your younger sister, Ivette, holds the power of compulsion and your older sister, Octavia, can move things with her mind. I've seen both in action. What I don't know is what power you have."

"What power do you think I have? You seem to be an inquisitive person. I'm sure you already have multiple guesses flying around in that head of yours."

"I do," I said as we made our way down a slight hill. "At first, I thought you could read minds. Now I'm not so sure. I think it's something different. Maybe you can feel what others feel?"

"Very perceptive of you." Julian grinned. "I'm an empath."

"Meaning you can feel people's emotions?" Violet asked. It was clear from the tone of her voice she didn't believe him.

"Exactly."

"That's a crappy gift to have, considering all of the

cooler ones out there," Violet said, and I found myself chuckling at her bluntness.

"I suppose you're right," Julian said. "I've often thought of it as a curse, but I imagine there are worse powers."

"Like?" I prompted, enjoying the topic.

"Like being able to hear others' thoughts," Julian insisted. "It's bad enough feeling the emotions of others, but I think it would be one hundred times worse if I could hear their thoughts instead. Nobody wants to know what someone else is thinking unfiltered."

I couldn't agree with him more. Mind reading was one power I never wanted to have. It seemed like a recipe for obtaining the worst migraine of your entire life daily.

"Why do you feel like feeling others' emotions is a curse? Seems to me like you got off easy in the scheme of powers," Violet said.

"Feeling someone's emotions is not getting off easy. It took me a long time before I was able to build a wall to block out emotions that were too overwhelming. Before that, I was a walking bipolar episode. Now, it's not as bad. I only tap into what others are feeling when it benefits me, or when I think I can help them in some way with whatever it is they're feeling."

A thought came to me. "Does it work with animals? Can you feel what they feel too?"

"I can. It's part of the reason I went to veterinary school. I've always loved animals, even when I was human, but once I learned to fine-tune my empathic abilities, I wanted to put it to good use. I learned early on I could pinpoint where someone's pain or discomfort was with a few touches and some focusing. What better way to put that skill to use than to give animals a voice and help them?"

"Well, yeah. But why not become a doctor? Like a doctor for humans? You could help so many people with your power," Violet insisted.

"Animals don't have nearly as many emotions as humans," Julian said. "Working with them instead of humans is sort of like a break for my brain."

I opened my mouth to say I understood, but someone yelling close by caused me to clamp my lips shut. It stemmed from somewhere to our right. While I couldn't tell who it was, I knew instinctively it wasn't Eli.

He was okay, but whoever I was hearing was not.

Chaos erupted nearby. The howls of my pack members had goose bumps prickling across my skin. My wolf demanded to be set free, but I refused to give in. I needed to see what was going on for myself first.

I broke into a run with Julian and Violet flanking me. As the three of us crashed through the woods to where the noises seemed to be originating, my heart beat triple time inside my chest. When we came upon the chaos, it nearly stopped because what I saw was something straight out of a horror film.

Wolves from the pack circled Dorian and Eli, who were crouched down on the ground, creating a wall of protection. From what? And who had been yelling? Dorian? My attention focused on him. He was definitely injured. Blood pooled around him, soaking into the ground and spilling outward. I had no idea where it was coming from though. My view was being blocked. I did see when Eli took off his shirt and wrapped it around Dorian's arm as the members of the pack circled.

"What happened?" I asked as I continued toward them.

Eli jerked to look at me, his eyes wild with fear. "Get out of here! Now! Julian take them somewhere else! The Midnight Reaper is here!"

Every inch of me went on high alert. My wolf nipped at my insides, begging to be set free so she could protect us. Dorian let out another howl of pain, and chills crept along my spine as I glanced around.

"He needs to be taken to Gran's," I said as my gaze shifted back to Dorian. He looked as though he could walk, but I worried the amount of blood he'd already lost might've diminished his strength, making it impossible.

The wolves of our pack widened their circle to include Julian, Violet, and me at Eli's command. I stepped closer to Eli. He was still trying to stop Dorian's bleeding.

"I know," Eli said through gritted teeth.

"Let me and Violet take him." I bent at the waist and maneuvered my way between Eli and Dorian, taking over. Eli's T-shirt fell to the side, and I was able to get a glimpse at Dorian's wound. His arm was mutilated. It looked as though someone had sliced him up with razors, filleting his skin in every direction while trying to sever his arm from his body in the process.

What the hell kind of monster were we dealing with?

"Be careful," Eli insisted.

Dorian made a noise as I secured Eli's T-shirt to his heaviest bleeding wound again. It sounded as though he was trying to say something, but his words were faint. I wasn't able to make them out through the pounding of my heart and the sound of my wolf snapping at me frantically.

"What did you say?" I asked, and then placed my ear next to his lips.

"Diversion," Dorian whispered. "We need a diversion."

"Can you create a diversion so Violet and I can get him out of here?" I asked Eli.

"I can," Julian insisted. "Give me a second to tap into the emotions lingering around here. I might be able to find where this vampire is and then rush him." He licked his lips and adjusted his glasses before closing his eyes. I had no clue how his powers worked, but I had faith he'd be able to do what he said. "When I tell you to go, go."

I locked eyes with Violet, making sure she was on the same page as me.

"Okay. We will," I said.

Eli helped us lift Dorian to his feet.

"Got him?" Eli asked Violet.

"Yeah," she said.

He looked to me next. My eyes locked with his, and I let everything I wanted to say to him pass through my stare. Eli mouthed *I love you,* and my heart fluttered.

"I love you too," I whispered as I prayed to the goddess of the moon we'd make it through this moment safely.

"Can the two of you please stop sending love notes through the air with your emotions? It's distracting me from what I'm trying to do," Julian snapped.

"Sorry," I said as I stared at him.

His eyes had remained closed, but his arms now hung slack at his sides. A more relaxed sense spilled into the air around him as his features seemed to soften. When his head tipped to the side, I knew he'd found what he was searching for.

"There you are," he whispered. "Well, aren't you an angry little vampire."

My heart kick-started as I prepared to run once Julian gave the signal. I glanced at Violet, making sure she was still ready. She nodded and my gaze drifted to Dorian. His face was clammy, and he looked as though he were on the verge of death, but even so, he nodded, letting me know he was ready as well.

"Go," Julian insisted with a hiss seconds before he rushed away in the direction of the vampire.

We didn't waste any time getting Dorian out of there. Both Violet and I knew we didn't have long before Julian's distraction dissolved and all hell broke loose again. When we were halfway to the clearing of the trailer park, warmth started to seep through the T-shirt pressed against Dorian's wound and dampened my hand.

His bleeding had picked up from all the movement.

Shit.

"We're almost there," I said, hoping he'd be able to hang on a little longer.

If he passed out or his knees buckled, Violet and I wouldn't be able to get him out of the woods. He was more than twice our size.

A growl echoed from somewhere deep in Dorian's chest. He had to be in serious pain, but I could do nothing to ease it. All I could do was focus on getting him to Gran.

Once we broke through the woods and into the trailer park the tightness squeezing my lungs eased, and I felt as though I could breathe again. Violet and I hurried toward Gran's trailer. There were no lights on when it came into view, but it wouldn't matter. Gran would wake the instant she heard someone at the door. If she didn't, Dad or Mom would. Gracie was a lost cause, being as sound a sleeper as she was.

When we reached the steps to the trailer, I propped Dorian against the railing.

"Just a second." I started up the steps.

My fist beat against the door while my heart palpitated in my throat. Someone needed to wake up, because Dorian was at risk of dying on Gran's steps if he didn't get some sort of treatment. I beat on the door again, this time louder.

Movement sounded from somewhere inside.

"I'm coming," Gran grumbled. When she swung the door open, her brows were knitted together and her eyes were sharp, but at the sight of me her features softened. "Mina? What's going on? Are you okay?"

"I'm fine. It's Dorian," I said as I motioned behind me to where he was slumped against the railing of the stairs. "He was attacked while on patrol."

"He's bleeding. Badly," Violet insisted in a shrill voice.

My gaze snapped to her. She looked ashen, and her eyes were wide. Beads of sweat dotted her upper lip and forehead. She was too young for all of this. Too young to be out this late and doing something so dangerous like helping us search for the Midnight Reaper.

What had we been thinking allowing her to be a part of this? She was only sixteen.

"Let's get him inside," Gran insisted as she stepped out of the way and motioned for us to enter the trailer. "Hurry. We need to get his bleeding stopped. He's probably left a trail of blood all the way to my front door."

My throat closed. I hadn't thought of that. I hoped whatever Julian had done to serve as our distraction had captured the Midnight Reaper's attention more than the scent of Dorian's blood.

I helped Violet get Dorian into the trailer. He could barely stand on his own any longer. He'd lost way too much blood. We started toward the couch, but Gran put up a hand to stop us.

"Don't set him down on my furniture until I have it covered up with something first," Gran insisted. "Let me get some old towels from the hall closet and a couple of trash bags."

She gathered towels from the hall closet and trash bags from beneath the kitchen sink while Violet and I stood with Dorian in the living room. Blood trickled onto the laminated flooring, and he groaned as his eyes rolled back into his head. He leaned on me a little more, and I wasn't sure how much longer I'd be able to hold up his weight.

When Gran came back, she laid out the trash bags on the couch and draped the old towels over them, doubling up so no blood would soak through.

"Okay," she said. "Get him situated."

Dorian made an awful sound as we maneuvered him toward the couch. I winced, hating we were causing him more pain.

"Sheila!" Dorian shouted at the tail end of his moan.

"Go get her," I said to Violet once we'd laid him down. "She should be here for this. She should know."

Violet nodded and headed out the door to retrieve Dorian's wife, Sheila. I felt bad for her, waking in the middle of the night to learn your husband had been attacked by something and was close to bleeding to death wasn't something I'd wish on anyone.

"Hold this here," Gran insisted as she passed me a clean towel to press against Dorian's wounds. "His were-wolf healing should kick in soon to help stop the blood flow."

She moved to the kitchen to riffle through her cabinets while I held the towel in place.

"Okay, here's what we're going to do," Gran said as she made her way back from the kitchen carrying a large bowl with steaming liquid and a roll of paper towels. "I need to clean the area so I can see what I'm dealing with. Go in the kitchen and bring me the herbs I set out on the counter. I'm going to need you to make a paste."

I nodded and headed to the kitchen where I gathered all the herbs. Only one of them looked familiar. Dried yarrow. I remembered it from when I was little and had seasonal nosebleeds. Gran would always make me shove a couple of dried petals up my nose to stop the bleeding.

It worked like magic.

I placed all of Gran's herbs on the coffee table and stared at the wounds on Dorian's arm. I'd been right before; it looked as though someone had taken razor blades to it, mutilating the skin. Was this what the other victims of the Midnight Reaper looked like? The ones that had been reported as having been mutilated? No wonder they'd stated the bodies were almost beyond recognition. If what I was witnessing on Dorian's arm was what the vampire had done to the entire body of those victims, it would definitely be hard to identify them.

My stomach twisted. I hoped Eli and the rest of the pack were okay.

"I know you're wanting to get back out there," Gran insisted as she looked up from wiping Dorian's wounds. It was clear my emotions were transparent from the way her brows furrowed. "But I need you to make me that paste first."

"Tell me the proportions," I said, wanting to make it fast so I could get back out there with the others. I didn't like not knowing what was going on. Had they already taken the vampire down? Had more pack members been hurt? Was Eli okay?

Gran pressed on an area of Dorian's arm that must've been sensitive because he let out a loud shout and came off the couch. The sound of it had Mom bolting down the hall and Dad not far behind. Winston started barking, and I expected Gracie to wake, but she didn't.

"What's going on?" Mom asked as she pulled on her robe and squinted her eyes, trying to make sense of what she was seeing. "Oh my God! What happened?"

"He was attacked by the Midnight Reaper while out on patrol," I said.

"Two tablespoons of this one, one tablespoon of this," Gran insisted as she pointed to two glass jars.

I reached for them and dumped the correct proportions into the tiny ceramic bowl I'd grabbed when I gathered the herbs.

"Is everyone else okay?" Dad asked. Worry for the pack flickered through his tone.

"They were when I left." My teeth sank in my bottom lip. I forced myself to focus on what I was doing and not think about what was happening in the woods.

"Obviously, Dorian is out for the count," Mom said. "I'll get dressed and head back out there with you. You're going to need a replacement for him if they're going up against whatever the hell did this."

"What? No," Dad insisted as he forced her to a standstill by reaching out for her wrist when she passed him. "You're not going out there. Look what this thing did to him. I don't want you anywhere near it. Either of you." His gaze drifted to me for a split-second before shifting back to my mother.

"I have to help. I can't sit here. It's not who I am anymore. Not in situations like this," Mom insisted. She held his stare.

"I'm coming with you, then," Dad said with conviction in his voice.

"No." Mom shook her head. "You need to stay here."

"If you're going out there with that monster, then so am I. End of story."

"No. You don't need to come. It's... it's safer for you to stay here," she said as she dropped her gaze to his cane.

"Because of this, right?" Dad asked as he motioned to himself and shook his cane.

"Now add in two pinches of this," Gran said, pulling me back to the task at hand. "A little water and mix it together."

Mom smoothed a hand across her face and sighed. "I'm sorry. I just don't want you to go out there and get hurt worse than what you already are."

"It seems as though we're at a standstill then, because I don't want you going out there and getting hurt at all," Dad insisted as he held her gaze. "I just got you back."

"I understand that. Trust me, I do."

"Then stay. Don't go out there."

Mom shook her head and licked her lips as she placed her hands on her hips. "I'm sorry, but I have to. Our pack needs me. I'm not the same person I was when I was abducted. I don't walk away from things like this anymore, and I damn sure don't hide from them."

"You never were that way. You were always strong." Dad narrowed his eyes. "But don't let that strength get you killed."

"I have to do this." She walked past him, heading down the hall to change.

My gaze drifted to my dad as I continued to make the herbal paste Gran needed. He looked heartbroken. Frustrated. Angered. I wanted to say something to him, but the right words wouldn't come. I wasn't sure there were any right words. Not for this situation when his manhood had been tested because of his disability.

"That looks good, Mina," Gran said. She held out Dorian's blood-soaked paper towels to me. "Take these to the trash can and get me the gauze and tape from the hall closet."

I did as I was told, maneuvering my way around my dad.

When I dropped the blood-soaked paper towels into the trash can, there was a knock at the door.

"Come in," Dad shouted, his voice laced with anger.

The door swung open, and Sheila rushed in looking hysterical.

"Oh my God! Oh my God!" She rushed to where Dorian was sprawled out on the couch.

"Calm down," Gran insisted as she smoothed on a thick layer of the herbal concoction to his wounds. "It looks far worse than it is. You know as well as I do his werewolf healing has already kicked in. That's the only thing that kept him from bleeding out. While some of the cuts seem superficial, others were straight down to the bone. He's lucky because I think the main goal of whoever is responsible for this was to sever his arm."

Gran's words had my stomach somersaulting. I reached into the hall closet for the gauze and tape. Mom came down the hall as I grabbed both items. She was fully dressed and ready to go.

"Let's go," she insisted as she pulled her hair into a ponytail.

I held up the gauze and tape. "One second. Let me give these to Gran."

I glanced at Dad as I walked past him. His eyes bounced from me to Mom. His jaw worked back and forth as he seemed to be debating whether to say anything more to either of us, Mom especially. We all knew once her mind was made up there would be no getting through to her. I understood that more than anyone because I was exactly like her. She was where I'd gotten my stubbornness from.

I'd never fully understood that until now.

"Here." I passed the gauze and tape to Sheila.

"Be careful out there you two. I don't want to have to bandage either of you up next, you hear me?" Gran insisted.

"You won't," I said even though I knew I couldn't promise her anything.

Mom nodded at Gran and then stepped to Dad's side. She placed a kiss on his cheek. "I love you."

"Love you too," he muttered without looking at her.

Mom glanced at me. "You ready?"

"As ready as I'll ever be," I said as I stepped to the front door where Violet stood. Fear reflected in her features. "You don't have to come. You can stay here, or you can head home. The choice is up to you."

Violet's teeth sank into her bottom lip. From the look in her eyes, it was clear she was debating what she wanted to do. "I think I'm going to stay here."

I nodded. "Okay. I'll be back soon."

"Be careful," I heard her say as I opened the door and stepped outside.

I'd be careful, but I wasn't sure it would do me any good going up against a monster.

18

"All right, take me to where the action is," Mom said as we stepped into the woods.

I opened my mouth to tell her it was before the lake, but sounds of the battle taking place between our pack and the Midnight Reaper echoed through the night. A strange hissing sound reached my ears next. While I'd thought of the vampire responsible for all of this as a monster before, hearing him hiss confirmed my theory.

"What the hell was that?" Mom asked as we neared the others.

"I think we're about to find out," I said, trying to keep hold on my wolf.

She desperately wanted free so she could get to Eli and the others faster than my human legs could carry me. She was ready to kick some ass. I held her back, though. Mom and I had a level of surprise going for us. Not even our pack would be expecting us to return. This was the only advantage we had, and I needed to make sure it was utilized properly.

That meant keeping my wolf in check.

Once we reached the scene, I'd decide if I needed to release her.

I stepped over a fallen branch and maneuvered through thick foliage until I broke into the clearing where the pack stood taking on the vampire responsible for all of this chaos. My eyes sought out Eli. He was in wolf form. Blood matted his fur in places, but it was difficult to tell if it was his or someone else's. Julian was beside him. Blood was splattered across his clothes and smeared along his face. His glasses were broken, and his eyes looked darker than I'd ever seen them. The rest of our pack seemed to be all over the place. Those who were willing and able to continue the fight stood behind Eli and Julian, while others lay nearby eerily still or just waking from a massive blow. Only one appeared to be hurt so badly he'd shifted into human form.

Tate lay on the ground a few feet away from me, motionless.

All the air rushed from my chest at the sight of him. Was he dead?

As I thought this, movement captured my attention. A female vampire stood in front of the pack members, poised and ready to fight. She was no taller than I was with short dark hair and a round childlike face. Dressed in all leather and a pair of stiletto heeled boots, she seemed like an assassin. Her hand reached out in front of her, and her fingertips grew stiff as though she were gripping something invisible too tight.

What was she doing?

When Eli's wolf cried out in pain as well as Julian and the others, I understood. She was using her power on them. Slicing them up with the invisible razors of her mind. The same ones she'd used on Dorian.

I could barely breathe as I watched. This chick was powerful. More powerful than anyone I'd ever encountered.

My gaze zeroed in on Eli. I watched as the cuts along his leg widened and deepened before my eyes seconds before they spread upward to the midsection of his wolf.

"No!" I shouted.

The vampire shifted to face me. She extended her other arm in my direction, and I felt the first flickers of white-hot knives slice across my left cheek. Moon magic filtered through the air, and I knew without looking at her, Mom was shifting beside me. The sight of another wolf must have distracted the vampire long enough for Eli to slip free of her hold. He launched forward and sank his wolf's sharp teeth into her neck. The female vampire let out a hiss of agony as she gripped Eli, but he refused to let her go. When he finally did, there was a gaping hole in the side of her neck. She fell to the ground, and her skin became papery as she turned to ashes like I'd watched other vampires do before.

Eli's wolf's eyes were on me. I could feel them.

I reached up and touched the place where the vampire's imaginary razors had sliced my cheek. The cuts burned, feeling like bee stings. Really pissed off bee stings.

A softness shifted through Eli's wolf's eyes. He was upset I'd been hurt. I could sense it.

"Glad that's over," Julian insisted as he took off his broken glasses and messed with their cracked lenses. "She was incredibly strong."

I stepped forward, wanting to get a better look at her. Her skin was translucent as she continued to turn to papery ash. There was no doubt she was dead, regardless of how strong she'd been.

Moon magic filled the air again. Eli and the rest of the pack shifted into their human forms.

"Are you okay?" he asked as he rushed to where I stood. His hands landed on my hips and he stared me in the eyes.

"Yeah, I'm fine. You?"

"I'm good," he said before shifting his attention to Julian. "Have you ever seen anything like her? Anyone who possesses a power like that?"

"No." Julian shook his head. "It was almost as though she wielded invisible razors. She also seemed hell-bent on killing you," Julian said as he narrowed his eyes on Eli.

"So, you think this was an attack on our pack?" I asked through gritted teeth.

I was sick of people trying to take us out. When the hell would we be left alone?

"Could be." Julian shrugged. He glanced over the vampire's body. "Wait a minute." His brows furrowed as he bent to look at something.

"What?" Eli stepped closer to Julian, trying to see what he saw.

I watched as Julian pulled back the vampire's top,

revealing a black marking beneath her collarbone. It looked like a tattoo.

"This is a branding. A Sire Brand," Julian insisted.

"You say that like it's something we're all supposed to know," Max said from behind Julian.

"Sorry. A Sire Brand is magical. Basically, it's a marking a vampire can place on other vampires in order to control them like a magical compulsion rune," Julian said as he continued to stare at the black mark. The sight of it seemed unnerving to him. "It's not something I've seen in a long time."

Again, skepticism pooled in my lower belly. Julian was hiding something.

"When was the last time you saw it?" I asked.

Julian glanced at me. "A very long time ago. And I would prefer not to talk about it."

Obviously, it was a sore subject. Didn't mean I planned to steer clear of it. He seemed to have information that might be important.

I opened my mouth to press harder, but Eli spoke before I could.

"So, that means this wasn't the Midnight Reaper? Instead, it was a soldier."

"Exactly." Julian stood. His gaze shifted to Eli. "The Midnight Reaper is more than one vampire. As you said, this was one of his soldiers."

My stomach somersaulted. This vampire had been powerful. Did the other vampires serving as soldiers for the Midnight Reaper harbor crazy dangerous abilities similar to this ones as well?

"Is there any way to track who the Sire Brand belongs to?" Mom asked.

Julian shook his head. "Unfortunately, no. There isn't a distinct mark for each Sire Brand created. They are all the same, only they're created by different vampires. That doesn't mean everyone is connected to one vampire though; it means they're all connected to the one who drew the rune on them."

"You said this was something you haven't seen a while," Eli said. "Does that mean it's something not common among vampires, then?"

"Yes. This is ancient. It's not something I've seen in well over a hundred years."

"Would that narrow it down any as to who could be doing this?" I asked.

There couldn't be that many ancient vampires roaming the earth, could there? And if there were, wasn't there a club among them so they could all brag about how old they were?

"I don't think so." Julian shook his head. "Vampires aren't normally close-knit. We're more solitary. Witches have their covens and wolves have their packs, but vampires don't stick together unless they're part of the same bloodline or an actual family."

"Is there any way we could get the Caraway witches to do a spell that might give us the knowledge of who placed the Sire Brand on this vampire?" Mom asked.

"It's possible they might be able to do something, if they had time before the body turned to ash," Julian said. He motioned to the vampire at his feet. "But I don't think time is on our side. She's nearly gone."

I glanced at the vampire. The wind picked up and bits and pieces of her blew away.

"I'm sorry. I wish there was a way to pinpoint who was causing all of this chaos, but there isn't," Julian insisted. "The only piece of advice I have left to give you is that when vampires have been Sire Branded to a particular vampire, they all travel together, which often means if you've spotted one there are others nearby."

Goose bumps pickled across my skin. Suddenly, I felt as though eyes were on me, watching from the woods somewhere.

"Judging from how badly we just got our asses handed to us," Max said. "I think we should consider retreating. It might not be wise to go against another one of these vampires while we're all beaten up and exhausted."

"You're right," Eli surprised me by saying.

Determination still festered through his bright green eyes, though. He wanted to keep going, that much was clear, but he didn't want to put our pack in any more danger than it already was. His gaze shifted around, taking in the state of his pack. When his face grew pale and his mouth dropped open, I remembered who was lying on the ground, motionless and in his human form due to injuries.

"Tate!" Eli shouted as he rushed to his brother's side.

My heart pounded in my chest as I watch Eli search for a pulse.

If his brother died tonight, Eli would never be the same.

"He's okay," Eli breathed.

I wasn't sure if his words were for himself or us. It didn't matter. They still brought a collective sense of relief through the pack and even Julian.

Julian stepped to where Eli hovered over Tate and helped lift him. We all sprang into action then. Within seconds, we were exiting the woods to lick our wounds.

The night hadn't been a total waste. We'd taken down one of the Midnight Reaper's soldiers. However, we had no clue how many more there were or what powers they possessed. I was positive we'd find out soon though because Eli wouldn't rest until they'd all been taken out.

19

The next day, those of us who are able went out to patrol again. It was an uneventful day, which was fine by me because I wasn't sure I was ready to go up against another of the Midnight Reaper's soldiers so soon. No one seemed to be except for Eli. I'd never seen him more determined.

By the time mid-afternoon rolled around, we'd opted to take a break for a couple hours and return once night fell. Eli wasn't happy about the break, but he understood the needs of his pack. We needed rest and nourishment. Plus, some of us wanted to check in on members who had been injured the night before and see how they were doing.

Dorian had been bandaged up good enough by the time we brought Tate and the others to Gran. She had had a long night mending everyone, but it wasn't anything she couldn't handle. Gracie had woke and helped as much as she could, and Violet had stayed to help too. Tate would be okay, but his injuries would take his wolf longer to heal than some of the others.

The scent of burgers grilling made its way to my nose as I stepped out of the woods and into the trailer park. I followed my nose until I spotted a large table in front of the party building. The Bell sisters stood behind it with drunken grins plastered on their withered with age faces. I wondered how many of their special drinks they'd had today.

In front of them was a tasty-looking buffet. Sheila stood beside the old women, filling a plastic bowl with chips. Dorian was nowhere to be seen. I imagined she had him laid up in their trailer, healing even though I was sure he was probably feeling much better.

"What's all this?" Eli asked when we neared the sisters and Sheila.

"A way to say thank you for what y'all are out there doing," Sheila insisted. She wiped her hands on a napkin and passed Eli a paper plate. "There's more than enough food here, so take what you want. We've got Philly cheesesteaks, hot dogs, and cheeseburgers."

As soon as she said hot dogs and cheeseburgers, I spotted my dad off to the side, manning the grill. It was good to see he'd found himself a place in all of this. A way to help. I knew it was important to him.

When we returned to the trailer park last night, I'd been unable to sleep and had slipped outside to gaze at the stars. I'd spotted him in front of Gran's with a bottle of whiskey in hand. He hadn't opened it, but it was clear from the look on his face he'd been in a dark enough place to. I was sure it was because the conversation between him and Mom earlier had made him feel worthless, even if that hadn't been Mom's intention.

When he slipped the bottle back into the bushes and headed inside the tension in my muscles melted away, but the pain in my heart lingered.

"Hey, sweetheart," he said when he noticed me staring at him. "Hot dog or cheeseburger?"

I shook my head. "No, I think I'll have a Philly cheesesteak."

"Suit yourself." He grinned.

A wide smile stretched across my face as he whistled to himself while continuing to flip burgers. I was glad he'd found something to busy himself with. He needed a purpose within the pack. Something to feel proud of himself for.

Manning the grill today was a good place to start.

"Everything looks delicious," Eli insisted as he glanced at the food covering the table.

"Oh, good," Violet said as she walked toward us carrying a case of water. "You finally came back. I was getting ready to send a text and let you know the food was ready."

"I think my subconscious knew there was something waiting," Max insisted as he took a paper plate from Sheila and reached for one of my Dad's cheeseburgers.

I accepted a plate from the oldest Bell sister and piled on barbecue chips before reaching for a Philly. I noticed Mom grab a plate and a hamburger bun before she headed to Dad at the grill.

"Are these your famous cheeseburgers?" she asked as she placed a kiss on his cheek.

"They are." He placed a burger on her bun and grinned.

I'd forgotten how much he enjoyed cooking. It had always been a passion of his. Something he had learned from Gran for sure. I remembered them taking turns cooking dinner during the week when I was little. Mom never cooked. I wasn't sure if it was because she didn't enjoy it, or if she didn't know how.

"I've missed your cheeseburgers," Mom insisted.

"I've missed cooking them." Dad flipped a burger high in the air and caught it on the spatula before placing it back on the grate of the hot grill. "I'd forgotten how much I enjoyed it."

"You used to love cooking. I'm surprised you put away your spatula for so long," Mom insisted as she squirted ketchup on the top part of her bun.

"I was in a dark place," he said without looking up from the grill.

I wondered if he was remembering last night and how he'd almost allowed himself to return to that dark place again. I hadn't mentioned anything to anyone about what I'd seen, not even Eli, because I felt it wasn't my secret to share.

Dad was happier today. Maybe it was because he was cooking, or maybe it was because he'd fought an old demon and won.

Either way, I was glad to see him smile.

Once I made my plate, I stepped to where Eli stood and ate. Gran came into view, followed by Gracie. It was odd to see her not with Cooper. From the basket Gracie was carrying, I knew she was helping Gran tend to the pack members who'd been injured in last night's epic battle again. I was glad to see her spend time with Gran, even if it was for something so horrible.

"Did you get another one today?" a soft voice asked, jarring me from my thoughts.

Jonas had come out of nowhere. He looked up at Eli, begging him to say yes.

Eli shook his head. "No. We'll get another one soon though. Trust me."

"I do." Jonas smiled.

Eli ruffled Jonas's hair. "Good. Did you get something to eat?"

"I had a hot dog."

"What? No chips?" Eli teased.

"I wasn't really that hungry," Jonas said with a shrug.

"I know barbecue chips are your favorite. There were some over there." Eli pointed to where the youngest Bell sister was dishing out giant handfuls of them. "Better get some before Ms. Bell passes them all out."

"Here, you can have some of mine." I grabbed a handful and held them out to him. "I got too many. I won't be able to eat them all."

"Thanks," he said as he grabbed them from me.

He crunched on one as he walked back to his trailer. The windows were dark, as though the trailer was in mourning. It had me thinking of June.

"How's your mom?" I asked Eli, knowing he'd taken a moment to check on her this morning before we began patrol.

"She's doing okay," Eli said before he took a bite of his Philly. "She's supposed to go to the funeral home tomorrow morning to pick up my Dad's ashes. It's got her all shook up."

His voice was cold and unfeeling as though he wasn't truly processing the words he was saying. In fact, I wasn't sure he'd processed his father's death at all yet.

"I'm sure," I said. "Does she need anyone to give her a ride? If so, I'd be glad to."

I still felt bad for not visiting with her sooner than I had.

Eli glanced at me, his bright green eyes glittered in the sunlight. "I love you."

"I love you too," I said, not understanding where his sudden declaration came from.

"You care so much about everyone in this pack."

I shrugged. "Doesn't everyone? We're family."

"Not as much as you," Eli insisted. "No. Mom doesn't need you to give her a ride because I'm taking her. I feel like I should, you know? I need to be there for her." His voice shook when he spoke, and I was glad to see an emotion besides anger surrounding his father's death trickle through him.

"I think it's great you're taking her."

"Thanks." Eli wiped his mouth with his napkin. "I'm thinking about making all of my brothers come. It's something we should do as a whole family."

"That's a good idea." I smiled. "I'll probably give Ridley a call in the morning while you're with your family to touch base and make sure the witches are still on track in putting up that ward."

Eli pulled me into him and placed to sloppy kiss

against my lips. "Beautiful, compassionate, and brilliant. How the hell did I get so lucky?"

"Oh, whatever," I said as I playfully slapped him away.

He grinned, and I felt like I'd won the lottery. The last few days Eli had turned into a hard, cold version of himself with everything that had happened, a version I didn't recognize. I knew it was because he was dealing with a lot, and I hated to see him seem so cold.

This smile, though. It was golden.

20

The full moon hung brightly in the sky. I wanted so badly to head out to the lake and meditate, but I knew the woods weren't someplace to go alone, more so now than ever.

Instead, I settled for a patch of grass between our trailer and Glenn and Taryn's. It wasn't ideal, but it was better than nothing.

I pulled in a deep breath for a count of one, and then exhaled for a count of three. After a few breaths, the tension in my shoulders eased, and my muscles relaxed as I soaked in the beautiful moon goddess's rays of light. Today had been difficult, but I knew tonight would be even worse. It would be emotional and heavy because tonight we said goodbye to our alpha.

Sadness crept through me. It was the deeply rooted kind, the kind you knew without a shadow of a doubt you wouldn't be able to shake free from no matter how hard you tried.

I lifted my face to the moon and closed my eyes, sending a silent prayer to the moon goddess, asking that she help me make it through the night, that she help all of us.

My cell rang, jolting me out of my thoughts.

I rushed to answer it, thinking it might be Ridley. She was supposed to call once her family had been able to set the ward in place. I hoped that was what she was calling me for now. I could use some good news.

"Hey," I answered.

"Hey. I hope I'm not bothering you," she said. "I just wanted to let you know we got the ward up."

"That's great. Thanks so much for letting me know. I think the news will have everyone resting a little easier tonight."

"There was a little difficulty though," Ridley said. "Something seemed to be fighting us."

My stomach somersaulted. "What do you mean?"

"Just that it should've been easier to set the ward in place than it was."

"What would cause issues? Could it be because there are more vampires in town than we anticipated?" I chewed my bottom lip.

"Not necessarily," Ridley insisted. "My aunt thinks there was some kind of magic at play. Something attached to the vampires."

The Sire Brand.

Shit. I'd completely forgotten about it. Since so much chaos had taken place between the last time anyone from the pack talked with the Caraway witches, I was positive they hadn't been informed of the new information about the vampires.

They had never been told about the Sire Brand.

It had slipped my mind the other day when I talked to Ridley, asking for an update.

"There was something called a Sire Brand attached to the vampire we killed in the woods," I said. "I'm sorry we forgot to mention it to you with everything going on."

"A Sire Brand? Like a special bond between a vampire and their maker?"

"No. This was explained to me as something more like a branding. Julian found it on the vampire we took out. She was part of the Midnight Reaper group, and she was vicious as hell. She had a crazy power where she could wield invisible razor blades. She managed to slice up a few of our pack members before we took her down."

"I'm glad you took one of them out, but did Julian happen to say what the Sire Brand was for? Or what it does?" Fear registered in her voice. "If it is too powerful, the ward we placed might not work. Just because it's up, doesn't mean it's strong enough to fight against something like that."

"Julian said it's a magical mark that makes vampires become compelled to do whatever the vampire who branded them wants. Basically, the vampire in charge doesn't have to share the ability of compulsion, all they have to know is a special rune. Once they have it on a vampire they want with the intent of them doing something for them, that vampire remains under their control until they die." I hoped that was everything Julian had mentioned about the strange mark. "Apparently, it's an ancient mark he hasn't seen in a long time."

"Damn it," Ridley whispered into the phone. I wasn't positive, but I was pretty sure it was the first time I'd ever heard her cuss. "The ward we put up might not stay in place. I'll have to talk to my aunt about this and get back to you. Julian said it was a magical rune, right?"

"Yeah. One from the middle ages."

"Hmm. I wonder if my aunt knows anything about it. If she does, we might be able to tweak the ward. If not...well, who knows what we'll be able to do to help the situation." Her voice lacked confidence, which had my stomach twisting into knots.

"I'll call you back later. If it happens to be too late, then I'll call you tomorrow. I know your pack is dealing with a lot tonight, and I don't want to bother you," Ridley said.

"Thanks." I licked my lips. "I'm not going to mention this to Eli. Not tonight. You're right, my pack is going through enough tonight. No one needs this added to their plate, especially not Eli. Please make sure your aunt doesn't contact him about this."

"I will. Why don't I go ahead and say I'll call you tomorrow instead of later tonight? I need time to look in to things and so will my aunt," Ridley said. The knots in my stomach began to unwind. It was nice to know Ridley was taking care of this for me, for us. "I really am sorry for your pack's loss. For Eli's and his family. Please let him know I'll be thinking of him tonight."

"I will," I said before I hung up.

A long breath expelled from my lips as I stood and

crammed my cell into my back pocket. When I stepped inside the trailer, Eli was sprawled across the couch with Moonshine on his chest. A TV show played on low in the background, but Eli wasn't looking at the screen. His gaze was fixed on the ceiling fan, watching as it spun.

"Hey." I closed the front door behind me. "Are you okay?"

"Not really," Eli said. Pain reflected in his tone.

I moved to the couch where he lay and positioned myself on the edge of the coffee table. My heart pounded. I didn't know what to say because I'd never had a parent die. I'd had one disappear for a few years, but this wasn't the same. It wasn't even close.

"Do you want to talk about it?" I asked, my gaze never wavering from him.

"My mind is going in circles. I can't believe we're saying goodbye to my dad tonight." His voice cracked when he spoke. "I really thought I'd have more time with him."

I stared at him, watching as his brows furrowed while he became lost in his thoughts. Was he thinking of the things he always thought they'd do together? Was he remembering past memories the two of them shared?

"I've been trying to remember what the last thing I said to him was," he said. "I know it wasn't what I wanted my last words to be to him."

"Say those words tonight," I suggested in a soft voice.

Eli swallowed hard. "I don't know what I'll say tonight." He smoothed a hand over his face and released a long exhale.

Tears swelled in my eyes as I stared at him. I couldn't

imagine the pain he was feeling. Same as I couldn't imagine one of my parents dying suddenly and me not being able to say goodbye.

"I didn't think I'd have to step up as alpha so soon. I thought I had years before that responsibility fell to my shoulders."

I placed a hand on his forearm. "I know. I'm here for you, though. You're going to make it through this. We're in this together."

The ghost of a smile twitched at the corners of his lips as his gaze shifted to me. "I know, and I love you for sticking with me," Eli said. "I just hope I can be half the alpha my dad was."

"You'll do fine. I'm sure he's already proud of everything you've accomplished the last couple of days."

"Maybe." Eli's stare drifted back to the ceiling fan. "I don't want to let anyone down. I'm worried I might not be as good of an alpha as he was to our pack, that I might not be able to handle the responsibility well enough. What if I screw up?"

"I'd say those are pretty damn normal fears to have." The words flew from my mouth without thought. They weren't anything Eli had expected me to say, but maybe that's why they brought a smile to his face when I didn't think it was possible.

Eli's lips formed a small smirk. "Pretty damn normal, huh?" he repeated.

"Well, yeah. I'm sure when your dad first became alpha he worried he'd screw up too. That's normal. It's also normal to screw up. I'm sure your dad did at one point or another while being alpha. It's what people do.

We make mistakes. Nobody's perfect. And the honest truth is, no one expects you to be either."

"Have I told you how much I love you?"

I laughed. "You have, but I'm always willing to hear it again."

"I love you, Mina Ryan," Eli said. "And there's no way in hell I'd be able to make it through this without you."

I leaned in and pressed my lips to his. "I love you too."

"Lie with us," he insisted as he moved over on the couch. Moonshine huffed and readjusted herself on his chest as though she were pissed with the movement. "Don't mind her. There's plenty of room," he said as he stroked behind her ears.

I snuggled into his side, grateful he was in a place where he wanted me close again. Closing my eyes, I pushed everything from my mind and focused on giving Eli all of my love because he was so damn deserving.

21

Eli's mom led the pack through the woods toward the lake. Everyone carried a paper lantern as we followed. The area had been searched minutes before by Dorian, who had healed up nicely, and a few other members of the pack.

It was sad we had to look for the Midnight Reaper group of vampires before we could say goodbye with a traditional ceremony to our beloved alpha.

My wolf howled in mourning once we reached the lake, and June spun to face us. A glass jar containing the ashes of Eli's dad glinted in the moonlight. Jonas, Micha, Cooper, and Tate, who still was a little cut up, flanked one side of June while Eli flanked the other. My gaze traveled over their faces, unable to linger long because the sight of their pain hurt me too badly.

"Thank you all for coming tonight," Eli said. "My father, Wesley Vargas, previous alpha of this pack, would be pleased to see each of you here tonight. It is in his honor we gather to say our final goodbyes." Eli's voice was strong and steady, but I knew him better than anyone and was able to decipher the emotion embedded in his tone.

Inside, he was barely able to hold himself together. This broke my heart.

"Tonight, we take the ashes of our alpha and release them into the wind, sending him back to the moon goddess and the Earth all at once. May his soul rest in peace. May his wolf roam freely. And may he always be remembered," Eli said as he nodded to his mother, letting her know it was time to release her late husband's ashes.

As she did, the entire pack glanced up at the full moon and said a silent goodbye to the alpha we'd known and loved. My wolf howled so loudly my insides vibrated.

"To the alpha," we each said in unison as we released our paper lanterns into the night sky.

Up against the dark sky, the lanterns shone like twinkling stars. They reflected off the rippling waters of the lake and gave a magical feel to the evening when mixed with the full moon, one I felt our alpha would have enjoyed.

I noticed when Eli wrapped his arm around his mother. His brothers leaned in closer to her as well. June's body shook as she pulled her boys in close. My heart broke for them.

It was a bittersweet moment.

Once Eli released his mother, he stepped to where I was and pulled me into him. He squeezed me close and buried his face into the crook of my neck. My arms wrapped around his neck as his warm tears soaked through my shirt.

"It's okay," I whispered. "Everything is going to be okay."

I knew the words might not mean much to him in the moment, but I felt the need to say them.

"I know," Eli said. "I can feel him. My dad's here with us."

"Of course he is. Who would want to miss this? Look how beautiful everything is," I said as I released myself from his grip and took a step back.

I glanced at Eli, watching as his profile became lit by the beautiful lanterns illuminating the sky.

"It is beautiful," Eli insisted.

Once all of the lanterns had disappeared from view, Eli gathered everyone's attention. I knew it was because he felt strong enough to announce himself as alpha. There was no doubt he would be accepted.

There was no one to challenge him; that wasn't how things worked within our pack.

Becoming alpha was hereditary. It was a birthright. It wasn't something to be won. We weren't barbaric. It was an honor to be passed down.

A hush fell over our pack as Eli opened his mouth to speak.

"Our pack has undergone immense tragedy over the last few years, but none greater than the recent loss of my father—the alpha," Eli said. His voice was clear and crisp as his eyes moved through the pack. "It is with great honor and brutal sadness I stand before you during this full moon to take my rightful place as the next alpha. As with the crowning of any new alpha, you each have a decision to make—do you accept me or do you not. If you accept, show me by changing. If you don't, you are free to go without any judgment."

Those around me wasted no time in shedding their clothes so they could complete the change. They accepted Eli. Of course they did. He was going to do great things as our alpha. I could feel it.

Once the pack had completed their shift, howls erupted into the night air.

"Thank you for your loyalty. I will do my best to serve this pack. I will try to live up to my father's name," Eli said. He glanced at the sky, and I knew he was making that promise to his father as well.

"And now we run," Eli insisted once his gaze shifted back to us. "We run in honor of my father and in remembrance of him, as well as in celebration of you accepting me as the new alpha. Thank you again for standing with me."

The pack howled out their approval as Eli stripped-down, proceeding to shift.

The cool night air ruffled through my fur as I watched him, thinking to myself how incredibly strong he was.

Once Eli had completed the shift, his bright green eyes locked with mine before he started through the woods. His movements were swift and laced with a sense of freedom. I wondered how much anticipation for this moment had coursed through him. How strong the desire to run was while he stood there talking to us?

He paused when he was a few feet away and glanced

back at me again. His head nodded, insinuating I join him. My mind cleared as I forced away all thoughts of the Midnight Reaper vampires lurking somewhere in Mirror Lake, the crumbling ward the Caraways had put up, the loss of our alpha and the gaining of a new one, Eli's heartbreak and sorrow reflected in his beautiful eyes–I pushed it all away and focused on the run.

THANK YOU

Thank you for reading *Moon Grieved*, I hope you enjoyed it! Please consider leaving an honest review at your point of purchase. Reviews help me in so many ways!

If you would like to know when my next novel is available, you can sign up for my newsletter here: https://jennifersnyderbooks.com/want-the-latest/
Also, feel free to reach out and tell me your thoughts about the novel. I'd love to hear from you!
Email me at: jennifersnyder04@gmail.com

To see a complete up-to-date list of my novels, please take a moment to visit this page: http://jennifersnyderbooks.com/book-list/

MINA'S STORY CONTINUES IN...

MOON REVEALED
Mirror Lake Wolves - Book Six

AVAILABLE NOW

Sometimes the enemy of your enemy becomes your friend...

With the help of a stranger her wolf doesn't trust, Mina learns the Midnight Reaper's identity. She also makes a deal with the newcomer, one Eli might not agree with.

But when the safety of the pack becomes a top priority and a secret about someone close is revealed, putting a friend in dire danger, priorities pivot.

The pressure is on in Moon Revealed, book six in the Mirror Lake Wolves series.

Please keep reading for a sneak peek...

CHAPTER ONE

"No, the bell peppers need to be chopped finer than that," I said as I leaned over Eli's shoulder.

He laughed. The rich sound of it vibrated through our tiny kitchen, bringing a smile to my face. I hadn't thought I'd get to hear him laughing so soon. I figured it would be weeks, maybe even months. Not because he was upset with me but because he was pissed with how unfair life could be.

We'd said goodbye to his father—our previous alpha —only last night.

"Says who?" Eli spun to face me while pausing in his chopping motion.

"Says the recipe." I flipped my phone around so he could see for himself. "In the picture it shows *finely* chopped bell peppers, not chunks."

"It's all preference." He flashed me a half smile that I noticed didn't reach the corners of his eyes but any semblance of happiness I could get from him I'd take. "I don't think they have to be paper thin and microscopic like in the picture. It'll still taste just as good with them a little bigger."

"Fine, but don't make them too big." I glanced at my phone, checking to see what the next step in the breakfast recipe was. I was glad I'd thought to go grocery shopping and get ingredients for something we could make together. It was definitely helping get our minds off things.

I wasn't trying to make Eli forget his dad. I was only trying to keep him from drowning in his emotions.

It seemed to be working.

"Okay, how's this?" Eli asked as he sliced another section of yellow bell pepper thinner than he had before.

"Much better," I said. "It looks more like the peppers in the picture."

"Good. See, my chopping skills are improving."

I kissed him on the cheek before hoisting myself up onto the kitchen counter. "That they are. I'll turn you into a cook before long."

"You mean your own personal chef." Eli winked as he flashed me another half-hearted smile.

He was trying. I was trying. However, I knew all either of us could think about was his dad and the fact that he was gone.

Eli was our pack's alpha now.

"I didn't say it. You did," I teased.

I reached for the onion and placed it near the cutting board so he would know it came next in the recipe.

"It's okay. I don't mind cooking for you," he said. "Someone has to make sure you eat."

"Oh, I would eat even if you didn't cook for me. Trust me. I'd cook for myself, but food always tastes better cooked by you. Nobody likes cooking for themselves. Everything always is better when someone else makes it for you. That's why so many people eat out."

A crooked grin twisted his lips. Satisfaction slithered through me. I would help get him through this one smile at a time. He'd be okay. I would see to it.

"I think you're wrong. People don't eat out because food tastes better when someone else makes it; they eat out because they're lazy," he said. He finished slicing the last bit of yellow bell pepper up before reaching for the sweet onion I'd set out.

"I can see that being true most of the time, but I really think it's because nobody likes to cook. For themselves. For anyone."

"What about the people working there? Don't you think they like to cook?"

I shook my head. "Not at all. They only cook because somebody pays them. There's a difference."

A rich, robust laugh burst from Eli. It was the best thing I'd heard in days. "Your dislike of cooking is hilarious. Makes me feel special knowing I was somehow able to get you to cook me grilled cheese and tomato soup once."

"I completely forgot about that." I grinned. "You should feel special. I don't cook for just anyone."

"I haven't forgotten about it at all. Now, I feel

prouder that I conned you into cooking for me." Eli wiggled his eyebrows. I leaned in to give him a kiss.

My lips pressed against his, and I felt like I was home. I reached out and laced my fingers through the hair at the nape of his neck. My body pulsed to life with desire, but I knew now wasn't the time to give in. Eli was hurting, even if he wasn't showing it, and I didn't want to take advantage of that. It didn't feel right.

I pulled back. My teeth sank into my bottom lip as I slipped off the counter. I retrieved a pan from one of the lower cabinets, and then placed it on the stove. After switching the burner to medium heat, I opened the fridge and grabbed the eggs. Eli was mute as he chopped the onion. He chewed the inside of his cheek, seeming consumed by his thoughts.

What was he thinking about?

When the question ate at me long enough, I opened my mouth to ask.

"A penny for your thoughts," I said, even though I'd always hated the expression.

Eli made a noise that sounded as though air were stuck in his throat. "Why do people say that?"

"I'm not sure where the expression came from, but I know people say it because they want to know what others are thinking."

He flashed me a no-shit look. "It's such an odd statement. You can't even buy anything with a freaking penny."

I cracked an egg into a bowl and waited for him to tell me what he'd been thinking. I knew all this penny talk was him stalling. Didn't he know I knew him better than that?

When I reached for the second egg, he made the same strangled noise as before.

"We should call it something else," he said. "I really can't stand that saying."

"Me either." I cracked another egg into the bowl. "What do you want to call it instead?"

"I don't know." He shrugged. "But it should be something better than that."

"Better than a penny?" I smirked. This was such a strange conversation.

"Yeah."

His dark brows pulled together. He was serious.

I focused on picking out a bit of eggshell that had slipped into the bowl while trying to think of something better than the penny analogy. Money seemed to be the only thing my mind could think of.

"How about keep the change?" I asked, thinking it was clever. Sort of like I was telling him to keep the penny since neither of us seemed to care for the saying.

"Keep the change," he repeated. "Actually, I like that."

I flashed him a small smile. "Me too."

I didn't backtrack to why the analogy had been said in the first place. Instead, I left it alone. I figured all of this talk about pennies and change had probably made him forget what he'd been so lost in thought about anyway. Maybe it was best I didn't know.

"So, what's the next step in the recipe?" Eli asked. "Anything else I need to cut up?"

"Umm, I'm supposed to whisk the eggs with a little bit of milk, spray the pan, and then we're supposed to add the veggies in along with a cup of cheese," I said as I reached for a fork because we didn't own a whisk. Our kitchen supplies were limited. "Then we're supposed to put a lid on it and let it cook for a few minutes without touching it."

Eli crept up behind me as I whisked the eggs with my fork. I could feel the heat of his body pressing against my backside. My thin sleep shorts and T-shirt were no match for his heat.

His woody, fresh scent, masculine and familiar, made its way to my nose. It had my knees buckling. My body wanted to melt against his, but I fought the urge. Eli brushed against me as he reached into the cabinet above the stove and grabbed the cooking spray. His hand rested on my waist, sparking my entire left hip to life. He seemed unaware of the inner turmoil he caused me.

After Eli sprayed the pan, I poured the egg mixture into it and stepped back so he could scrape the vegetables in before I sprinkled the dish with cheese. This was the first time since I moved into his trailer we'd cooked together. I had never made omelets before, but I'd eaten them often at home. Gran always made the best ham and cheese ones.

"And now for the lid," Eli said as he scraped the last little bit of vegetables into the eggs. He headed to the sink to rinse off his cutting board and knife.

I grabbed a lid that was a little too big for the pan we were using and covered our omelet.

"Now, we wait," I said as I hoisted myself back up

onto the counter. My eyes dipped to my phone as I read the instructions once again, hoping we weren't missing any steps. "Crap."

Eli dried his hands on a dish towel. "What?"

"We forgot to add three tablespoons of salsa." So much for our southwestern omelet.

Eli tossed the dish towel on the counter and headed for the fridge. "It's okay. We can just add it on top."

I opened my mouth to tell him that would work, but his phone rang. It echoed through the otherwise silent trailer, startling me. My gaze drifted to the clock on the stove. It was just after eight in the morning.

Who could be calling this early?

My stomach dipped. I had a feeling they weren't calling with good news.

Eli headed to the living room where his phone was on the coffee table.

"Hello?" he answered. "Hi. Yeah. Good morning to you too."

My brows pinched together. His tone was off. Why did he sound so surprised by whoever was on the other end? Hadn't he glanced at his caller ID before answering?

"Okay. I can round everyone up," he said, causing my stomach to flip-flop. "Thanks for calling. I'll see you in a little while."

Eli shifted his gaze to me once he hung up.

"Who was that?" I asked.

"Rowena Caraway."

The flip-flopping in my stomach intensified tenfold at

the mention of her name. Why would she be calling? And why so early in the morning?

The ward.

I'd nearly forgotten my last conversation with Ridley in light of everything else. She'd mentioned they were able to put the ward in place, but that it had been difficult. We assumed it was because of the Sire Brand runes set in place on the Midnight Reaper group of vampires that had made it difficult.

Ridley was supposed to call me with news on the rune and an update on the ward. She was worried, same as Rowena, it might not hold. Had something happened overnight, or was Rowena calling to wish Eli congratulations on becoming the new alpha?

"What did she say?" My voice quivered when I spoke. I cleared my throat, hating my nerves had betrayed me.

"She said she wants to meet this morning to discuss some things."

"Things involving the ward?" I asked even though I knew that had to be it.

"Possibly. She said I should ask my second-in-command to be present, as well as anyone else I'd like to keep informed when it comes to the Midnight Reaper vampires."

My heart lodged in my throat. Something must have happened. Whatever it was it couldn't be good if Rowena was calling a meeting.

AVAILABLE NOW

ABOUT THE AUTHOR

Author
Jennifer Snyder

Jennifer Snyder lives in North Carolina where she spends most of her time writing New Adult and Young Adult Fiction, reading, and struggling to stay on top of housework. She is a tea lover with an obsession for Post-it notes and smooth writing pens. Jennifer lives with her husband and two children, who endure listening to songs that spur inspiration on repeat and tolerate her love for all paranormal, teenage-targeted TV shows.

To get an email whenever Jennifer releases a new title, sign up for her newsletter at https://jennifersnyderbooks.com/want-the-latest/. It's full of fun and freebies sent right to your inbox!

Find Jennifer Online!
jennifersnyderbooks.com/
jennifersnyder04@gmail.com

CPSIA information can be obtained
at www.ICGtesting.com
Printed in the USA
BVHW031259311218
536789BV00001B/50/P